A RIVER WIDE

AMANDA J. MCGEE

PRAISE FOR A RIVER WIDE

"An Appalachian murder ballad for the twenty-first century, Amanda McGee's nail-biter of a novella shows us why it's dangerous to be a witch and dangerous to cross one. At the same time, *A River Wide* overflows with joys and sorrows that arise from the deep blood ties of family, drawing from profound wells of grief and hope to brew a ghost-haunted spell."

— MIKE ALLEN, WORLD FANTASY AND SHIRLEY JACKSON AWARD-NOMINATED AUTHOR OF *TRAIL OF SHADOWS*

"Like Alice Hoffman's *Practical Magic,* and Amal El-Mohtar's T*he River Has Roots,* Amanda J. McGee's novella *A River Wide* taps the bonds of sisterhood, survival, and power, and floods the senses with river water and witchcraft. McGee's characters have a deep, Dillard-esque, and—dare I say—holy bond with the Appalachian landscape, which can be capricious, cruel, generous, or tender in turns, much like the prose itself. *A River Wide* wanders deftly into various creeks and hollows of genre: thriller, ghost story, romance, family drama, and a middle-of-life coming-of-age. It moved me, deeply."

— C. S. E. COONEY, WORLD FANTASY AWARD-WINNING AUTHOR OF *SAINT DEATH'S DAUGHTER*

"*A River Wide* pulled me in with narrator Rhia's vivid voice, a small town's secrets, and a kind of elemental witchcraft I hadn't seen before. Rather than bend water to her will, Rhia must work with it, sometimes even bargain with it—and she can't take that lightly, even when what she's bargaining for amounts to her sister's life. I hope McGee has more plans for the witches of the Blackburn family and the Appalachian home they so lovingly, so precariously, inhabit."

— LAURA BLACKWELL, SHIRLEY JACKSON AWARD-WINNING AUTHOR

CONTENTS

This is a work of fiction. All of the characters, organizations, and events portrayed are either products of the author's imagination or used fictitiously.

A RIVER WIDE

Edited by Holly Lyn Walrath.

Cover art by Dante Luiz.

Cover Design by Holly Lyn Walrath.

Published by Interstellar Flight Press, Houston, Texas.

www.interstellarflightpress.com

ISBN (Print): 978-1-953736-63-5

ISBN (EBook): 978-1-953736-62-8

First Edition: 2026

To the waters of Appalachia.

CONTENT WARNINGS

This book contains murder, violence towards women, suicidal ideation, moments of anti-LGBTQ sentiment, and, obviously, death.

A River Wide

CHAPTER ONE

THERE IS blood in the grass and turned-up earth, but no Amey.

"Shit," I say, kneeling. Mud and blood on my jeans, but they were done for the day anyway. I've been sweating at the farmer's market for hours, and I don't know what happened here except that it was something bad, because I can feel that. Earth is, has always been, opaque, but blood is like water, and water always speaks to me. It's chicken blood, I can taste that much on the back of my tongue. No chicken, but so much blood and feathers, the thing is probably dead. It looks like Roy, the rooster. Green-blue feathers the length of my forearm are mixed with whites and browns. Roy is her favorite, follows her around like a dog.

Where is Amey?

I splay my hands over the dark soil, the rich, fluvial stuff of riverbeds and lake bottoms. Once, when we were teenagers, a boy put gum in Amey's hair, and Gran had to cut it off. No money for a hairdresser, so Gran did our hair. She was usually good at it, but the gum was so high up she had to cut off too much, and Amey's red curls had puffed up without the weight. She'd looked like a bobble-head doll. I made the mistake of saying as much. She ran out and hid in the earth of the backyard all night, with nothing I or Gran could do to get her out. Earth is her element. She hasn't done that in years, though.

Is it warmer here than elsewhere in the yard?

Is it breathing?

"Shit," I say again. The word slips out of me as if it's the only one I know. I can feel something down there, but the mud in between me and it makes it hard to tell. It could be Amey. Must be. Who else would be in my yard?

My cousin is one of those firecracker sorts of people, all emotion, and she's been upset lately. I don't know why. It doesn't do any good to ask her about things until she's ready to tell them. But with this much blood, Roy is dead. Even if she hadn't been chewing on something already, that would set her off.

Probably a raccoon or a neighbor's dog got him. I stand, wipe the dirt onto my jeans. Back Creek runs just feet from here, shaded by the trees. It's a small stream here, about ten feet across, but deeper than you'd think. I shield my eyes, stare out towards the water. It bubbles dully—not up, not angry, but there's a twang to it I can't place. I look for the drooping flags of purple iris, the flowers I dread the most, but find none. My breath sighs out in relief, even though there's a storm in my gut saying I shouldn't relax just yet.

I force it down. A dead rooster is enough of a crisis. No need to borrow trouble.

"Let her up when you can," I say to the yard, knowing it is listening. I can't sense much about earth, but that doesn't mean it can't hear me when it wants to. I run a hand through my short black hair. It's still muddy. I swear again, and turn to go back inside, feeling my skin crawl with unease I can't pin down.

Has someone else been here? Everything feels off, like there's eyes pinned between my shoulder blades. Amey will know more when she's ready to talk, so I head back up to make lunch.

We live well off the main road, in a patch of woods that's dense and good-sized enough to discourage casual visitors. This time of year, the leaves are still green but spotted brown and yellow. They've lost their newness. In the next week or two, they'll start to turn, but for now, they cling to the last dregs of summer, fighting the chill already lingering at night. It's just Amey and me out here, and Gran down the drive. It's better that way. We like our privacy.

The house is perched at the top of a slight incline—just out of the floodplain. Even a water witch knows better than to build too close to the creek, and I, of all water witches, know the creek is restless and angry when it wakes. Kind of like me, really, which is probably why we get along so well. Back Creek floods at least once every spring, usually more than that, but at least once that counts. I've seen it high enough to kiss our floorboards on a bad year.

Steep steps take me up to the deck, a new addition. I haven't gotten to staining it—the wood's still curing. I run my hands along the banister I carved with sliding, driftwood shapes. Amey sank the posts for the deck, sank them deeper than any slight woman should have been able. No concrete, though. That requires digging bigger holes, and even though she lets me dig for the garden, she doesn't like to cut into the earth that way. Maybe the deck will hold in the next flood anyway. If it doesn't, me and Back Creek will be having words.

Amey is a slip, and I'm mostly muscle with some curves thrown on. We live well out in the woods and mind our own business, but the funny thing about private property in rural America is that people shout a lot about the sanctity of it and then don't respect it much. Most people don't bother us, though, on account of them knowing that I, at least, am something strange. Amey's the normal one, but normal isn't always a blessing. If anyone ever finds out just how strange we both are—well, no one will buy my furniture anymore, that's for sure. I'll have to take it to the city market, an hour down the highway. I'd been meaning to anyway—the nearby town doesn't have enough people to keep me in operation by itself, even with the odd jobs I pick up from time to time and the eggs and tomatoes I sell. There's money in the bank from Amey's work at the bar, but if she's got something weighing on her, it's as likely to do with her work as anything. I may be the only breadwinner for a while.

I guess that's what family's for.

There's no point in wrestling my boots off, so I track some mud into the kitchen. It'll clean off the vinyl easily enough. I make a sandwich, glancing out the back window every few minutes. She doesn't usually stay under this long. The worry creeps up like the beginnings of a flood. I push it down again, head outside, and settle into the porch chair to wait. I try not to be angry at my sister by raising, who is not built for this world. Not that any witch has ever been.

There are birds singing, and I'm bone tired from a long day at the market, tired enough my eyes droop. Market days start before dawn, even in the summer, and it's already after lunchtime. Amey usually has lunch out before she heads to work in the afternoon on Saturdays, and I usually handle dinner. The absence of said lunch is why I'm out here in the first place, looking to see what she was into.

Our routine works, and we don't deviate from it without communicating. I haven't heard a thing from Amey since she left for work last night.

The sound of the water in the creek changes, and my ears prick up. I see red leaves on the baby maple that lists, reedy and waterlogged, on the other bank, a warning clear as hazard lights in the bright afternoon.

"Shit," I say, and if I didn't mean it before, I mean it now. The ground rumbles and spits.

What my backyard chucks up is not my cousin Amey. He is a man, or was, because this fellow is dead.

I waste a few minutes on panic.

The roiling earth is all deep brown mud, wet and clinging. I can't see who my yard has spit out. My feet slip and stumble on the stairs. There's no point in rushing, but adrenaline doesn't seem inclined to let me go slow, and I hit the concrete pavers at the bottom of the stairs with a teeth-clacking jolt. I've kept my feet, and they carry me to the dead man's side.

Randy Higgins is lying dead in my yard, mud caking his scruffy beard and round cheeks. For a moment, I just stand there staring.

He looks awful pale, beneath the mud. Like a whiter sort of clay.

Randy's a no-good scoundrel, but he's not the kind of man who would work up the nerve to stumble into our yard uninvited, not alone. And I know Amey didn't invite him—she says he's handsy at the bar. Which means there are two people missing from this tableau—Amey and whoever Randy was hanging around with when he decided to stir up trouble.

Can't have been dead long, the ground was still warm.

The corpse's mouth opens. A sigh comes out like a sea. I shriek.

"Jesus Christ, Randy," I say, then clamp a hand over my mouth. No witch should speak to the dead, except to say her goodbyes. It gives them ideas.

I hold my breath, but Randy doesn't do anything else. Thank God for that. The creek is rushing and whispering, and I can feel my heart rushing with it.

I have no idea how I'm going to hide the body, but I'm sure as shit going to have to because if Amey is still alive, I can't let her get locked up, and Randy is Eric's cousin, and Eric's on the force—but what if she's already locked up, what will I do then? I don't know where she is, and the water rushes faster, and if I don't calm down, I'm going to call it out of the banks on top of everything else, maybe even wake up things best left asleep, but Amey—

I take a deep breath. The creek calms a little.

First things first.

I get a tarp.

I'm not a little woman, but Randy is a heavy son of a gun, and our yard is steep. It takes me close to an hour to get him into the back of the truck. The only sign I've been handling a corpse is the crushed grass and mud. I've bound his blood inside him, which will only work as long as his spirit doesn't get any ideas about vengeance or what have you. You've all heard the stories of the corpse suddenly bleeding when the killer walks into the room. They're true, as you might imagine. Spirits still have a little control over their corpses, if they're mad enough. As mentioned, though, Randy's never had an original thought in his life.

Death's hardly the time to go changing yourself. The opposite, really.

The truck starts with its customary rattle. It's an old green 1975 Ford F-150, the last thing my grandfather drove before he died, and I inherited it along with everything else we own. I'm not going far, but I take the time to cover Randy in his tarp burrito with an old metal washing pan. I myself usually use washing pans for washing vegetables, but in this case, the shape serves to obscure the telltale lumps of a dead body. It won't pass more than a casual inspection. I also add a bag of mulch and one of chicken feed. I haven't seen hide nor feather of any of our chickens since I got home, so whatever happened here scared them bad. They'll come home at dark.

Or they won't.

I may not know what happened to saddle me with all this mess, but I know someone who knows more than I do. He's dead in the back of my truck.

My gut says I need to get a handle on that, fast. I hit the gas, and the truck lurches out of its parking spot and into the gravel driveway. I turn away from the main road, deeper into the woods. Every lump in the driveway rattles my cargo and makes my stomach clench.

Gran knew I'd be coming. She has a sixth sense about these things where Amey and I are concerned. She's in her rocking chair peeling apples when I pull up. It's apple time, and that makes me even more nervous to have a body to deal with because apple time is spirit time. Spirits are always harder to control when the apples come ripe, and the world slides a little closer to death. Randy will be no exception, for all he isn't the most strong-minded individual. Wasn't, I guess, since he's dead. I hope Gran can handle it.

Gran's trailer is at the end of our long driveway, which gives us all a bit of privacy now that we're grown, but not so much that we can't see each other. The trailer isn't big, just a little single-wide affair with white and brown vinyl siding sitting on cinderblocks and a wooden porch slapped on the front. Most days, Gran comes down for dinner with Amey and I, usually walking the gravel drive with her cane in her right hand and a pie in a bag on her left arm. Gran can bake, even though she's mostly blind. We figure both the baking and the blindness run in the family. I personally find kneading soothing, a good way to keep my hands moving when I need a break from the woodshed. Amey always complains about all the sweets we have in the house. Says they'll go to her figure, but that girl burns calories faster than the evangelists burn books, and she's only about as big around as a toothpick anyway.

I turn off the truck and lean my head against the wheel to still the babbling in my brain. Worry for Amey rises up like a wave, choking me.

"You've got yourself company, Rhia," Gran says. She hardly raises her voice, but the wind brings it to me anyway.

I make myself pop open the truck door and slither out onto the gravel drive with all the grace of a calf falling from its mother. The adrenaline is ebbing, fickle thing, and I feel tired, tired enough to fall through the floor of the earth.

I walk to the tailgate instead and hitch it down.

"Amey's gone," I say to Gran. "I found him in her place."

The old woman sits her peeling to the side. I can see her squinting at me, rheumy blue eyes straining. A wind rustles the trees, sighing out in time with Gran's breath.

"Leave that and come up on the porch," Gran says as I reach for the washbasin. "I'll get you some iced tea. Seems like you might need it."

I let my hand fall gratefully. No one likes looking at a dead man. Randy isn't my first, but I'm not in any hurry to get up close and personal with him again.

Gran has long white hair she wears in a braid down to one side. It used to be black, like mine, and it is straight as an arrow, like mine. We've all got blue eyes, her, Amey, and I, but Gran's are nearly white now with cataracts and the disease that makes her blind. They were always brighter than mine, which edge to darker shades. Amey has a mole in her eye, which is how Gran knew she'd be an earth witch long before the rest of us figured it out. Then again, that's the kind of thing spirits can tell you, and that's what a wind witch does, commune with the spirits—not just the big ones, but the little ones that flit about and nestle in the cracks, the ephemera of human beings. It's why I've brought Randy's body, instead of stashing him somewhere already. Somewhere no one will find him and bring the cops to my door.

Gran has gone inside, and I sink gratefully into a rocking chair, pressing through my toes to lean it as far back as it will go so I don't have to look at my truck. There have always been two chairs on this porch, ever since we moved her here. When Gran steps back out, the screen door swings closed with a clack behind her. She hands me the tea, condensation already beading on the glass, and she sits, then takes a deep gulp of her tea. The sound of her rocking is soothing. I lean forward, elbows to knees, cradling my glass. I'm studying the condensation and trying not to think about the dead man in my truck, even though it's hitting me all over again. Trying not to think about Amey.

"Breathe deep, girl," Gran says, like she can hear my heart rabbiting, "and lay it out for me."

I breathe deep, taking the air in through my nose, up behind my eyes, down through my belly. Exhale. Do it again for good measure, because I can see that the tea is shaking, which means my hands are, too.

"I came home and I found Randy Higgins dead in the yard. In the yard, deep." I take a swig of my tea, wish that it was something stronger. Remind myself that I don't drink anymore, and certainly not to deal with trouble.

"Tell me about the yard," Gran says, steady. She's always been steady, and the dead don't scare her, not when she's met so many of them. Gran says wind witches have to be steady because the wind isn't. She's had a long time to build herself up like a big tree, and I'm a vine clinging to the bark, desperate not to fall.

I tell her about the yard. Blood, chicken feathers, but no chickens to be seen. Upturned earth, warm in the shade, like a body. The way the creek had been restless. The blooming red of maple leaves, but no drooping purple flags of wild iris. Amey alive, but gone. A dead man where she should have been.

Gran is silent at the end of it, rocking and sipping her tea. I'm not shaking anymore. Water flows downhill. Fills the shape it is given. I do a lot of things to keep me grounded, gardening and baking and carving my tables. To keep the creek bound up inside, to ignore the calling of the bigger spirits, to keep one foot on shore. None of those things will help me here, I think.

"Amey buried him, surely," I say. Buried, not killed, because it sounds better, and I love my sister. Amey and I are cousins by blood, but we're sisters in every way that matters, and she needs me. I can feel it in my bones.

"Then he'll know where she's gone, probably," Gran says.

The wind flows again, and I catch the out-of-season smell of lilacs. Next to me, Gran smiles.

"Don't you worry, Archie," she says.

Not to me. Lilacs mean only one person.

My grandpa was a water witch, too. Just the dowsing kind, no visions like me. He died when I was a baby, but Gran talks to him all the time. She says she used to could see him, a washed-out blue photograph of a man who would always be wearing his favorite suspenders, forever. Now she can't see much at all, but she can hear the dead and feel the cold of them.

"I know to be careful. You'd think I'd never talked to a dead man before." Gran's voice is mild enough, for all that it's a rebuke. She gets to her feet. I hurry to help her down the stairs, and she shoos me away.

"Don't you go fussing over me, too. One of you is enough. I'm not made of spun sugar." She steps down the stairs, leaning on her cane. The wind picks up, rubbing the tree branches together. They squeal and slap.

"Randy Higgins," Gran says when she reaches my truck. Her blue dress has flowers as white as her hair on it, and it billows in the wind, a sharp contrast to the dark green of my old Ford. "What have you gone and done with my granddaughter?"

There is a thump from the truck bed, and a moan. The tea goes sour in my stomach. Waking up the new dead is so, so easy, and that's not the first time he's been called by his name.

"Now you get out of that body, Randy," Gran says, and she reaches out with quick, thin fingers and plucks at the tarp where it moves. There's a scent of old mud and lilies. The body stills, thank God, and there Gran stands, her hand caught in something that I only know is there by the tension in her arm. Wiry old muscles stand out beneath her skin.

"Say it so Rhia can hear now," Gran says, her voice stiff, and wonder of wonders, if I don't hear Randy Higgins on the wind.

"You get your hands off me, you old hag," says Randy, which is par for the course where Randy is concerned. Death ain't changed his manners. Gran gives a little twist of her wrist, like shaking out a sheet.

"Now, Randy," she says, "that is no way to talk to your elders."

"What'd you do?" His voice is cautious now. It's like hearing a conversation on speaker phone, and if I tell myself that's what Gran is doing, I can talk to him.

"Never you mind that," Gran says. She holds out her free hand to me, dropping her cane, and I take it. It's easy to give her a little of my own magic. She's family, and I have the creek to bolster me, which it doesn't mind doing right now. It's just a matter of setting my soul to *open* instead of *closed*. The rush of it passes through my palm and into her, and suddenly Randy is standing in front of me.

He's about the same as his body was, in the blue tones the dead wear. His belly is a little slimmer, but ghosts do that sometimes, looking more like they imagined themselves to be. He's got a camo tee shirt on that someone gave a collar for some godawful reason, and soft blond curls that made him quite a catch when he was sixteen and hadn't gotten into drinking quite as much, but now just make him slightly less unappealing. He leers at me, thumbs in the loops of his jeans.

"Hey, Rhia," he says. "Cursed anybody lately?"

I roll my eyes. Randy and I went to middle school together. Katie Miller, the most popular girl in school, had dumped my bag on the floor just for fun, and I had told her, quietly and with more composure than I should have had, that she would regret it. Then I had gone home and forgotten about it. Nothing would have probably come of it except that Amey had seen what happened and didn't care for it. I didn't realize she had whipped up a curse until she had already fed Katie's picture to the earth in the backyard. There hadn't been enough power in it to do more than give Katie a stomach bug and the worst breakout in Mattock County history, but everyone remembered what

I'd said and treated me strange for a while, and Gran tanned Amey's hide.

Katie still looks at me funny, at the market. Her husband plays guitar and sings every Saturday, and she's usually got her kids with her, and she makes sure they don't ever visit my booth.

"Where's Amey? And what were you doing in my yard?"

Randy looks mulish. "I wasn't doing nothing. Amey had it coming. Should have known better, Jack said."

My blood goes cold. I know who he's talking about. Jack Higgins is trouble and everyone knows it.

"What did you do to her?"

"I ain't telling you nothing," Randy says.

I exhale, push a little bit more of my power into Gran. She takes the hint. Randy flickers, like, and suddenly he's a lot more talkative.

"Now hold on, y'all, hold on just a minute," he says, face gone fearful. I don't know what Gran's done, but whatever it is, he doesn't like it.

"Only person who can hurt you now is Gran," I tell him. It's not a threat, really, just an observation, and Randy seems to know it because he wilts a bit, if a ghost can be said to wilt. I feel relief, a warm release in my chest.

"All I know is that Jack wanted to send her a message. He told me she loved her chickens, so I killed that rooster, and she saw me and came out screaming, and then the earth opened up and swallowed me."

I relax further. Maybe Amey just got scared and ran off. That's manageable. I'll find her and we'll figure something out.

That relief vanishes at Randy's next words.

"Probably scared Jack white," Randy says, with a little chuckle. "Wish I could have seen his face."

"Jack was there?"

"Sure. It was his idea, wasn't it?"

My hand tightens in Gran's, and we share a look of horror.

Randy's dead. Amey killed him. And Jack Higgins, the crazy sonofabitch, saw it all.

CHAPTER TWO

Every community has a mix of folks who call it home. Mattock County is no exception. You get poor folks and not-so-poor folks, white folks and brown folks, religious types and those that don't truck with that. You get folks who move away, more of those every year around here, and those whose roots go so deep we can't leave, like Gran and Amey and me. Amey's seen what happens when a witch tries to leave her patch of earth, and my mother got out, but not all of a piece as it were. Communities are made up of all kinds, that's their nature, even when there seem to be less differences than more.

And in every one of the places you go in the world, there will be a Jack Higgins.

Randy's mother was a Marshall, which is where the relation to the law comes in. He comes from a long line of law-abiders, but that breeding couldn't hold when it got mixed up with Higgins blood. Still, Randy came out mostly stupid and occasionally decent. Stupid people aren't harmful in and of themselves. It takes someone to shape them, someone with more than a lick of meanness, which requires imagination. The two traits aren't always mutually exclusive, but they're not often mixed up in the same body either. This was not the case for Jack Higgins, who was born only marginally bright, more than your average clever, and meaner than a striped snake.

Everything I knew about Jack came from Amey. He's frequented Spike's, the bar where she works, every Friday and Saturday since he got out of jail a few years ago. He has to have some money because he always runs up a tab, and he always pays it. Amey thinks the money's from drugs, or maybe more nefarious dealings. You'd think someone would have put the man away, seeing as he has a temper and a habit of hurting people, but aside from his one stint in the jailhouse a few years back, Jack seems to operate by rules that other people don't. I'm not surprised he thought he could get away with killing Amey's chickens.

"I'm sorry you're dead, Randy," I say to the ghost in my Gran's front yard. Shock is settling in. We both know better than to get caught, know better than to do what Amey did. I let go of Gran's shoulders. The porch steps seem as good a place as any to sit and put my head in my hands, so I do. Moving all that magic has left me winded, even this close to my creek. I'm not like Amey, a power, using my magic all the time. I'm just Rhia, plain, wide-hipped Rhia who likes to tend her garden and make things out of wood. I've got my divining and my creek and no interest to speak of in witchery outside of making sure the rain comes when we need it.

Gran is saying something to Randy, low-like, soothing. I've seen her send spirits on before, and it's a private thing, so I don't try to hear.

"Go in peace, Randy Higgins," she says, old voice young suddenly, and the wind sighs through the trees, and the ache of the newly dead eases out of my bones, and we're alone.

Well, there's still a body in the truck to bury, and Amey to find, and my heart seesawing about my chest like a tree about to break in the wind.

"Jesus," I say, hands in my hair now, pulling tufts of it up like a little forest. I wrestle with the urge to scream.

Then I stand up, because Gran needs to get back in her rocking chair and rest, no matter how tough she is. Talking a spirit away ain't light work, and I can't remember the last time she did it. In the aftermath, she looks frailer, small and tired. She puts a hand on my elbow as she comes even with me, and I help her up the stairs and get her settled. I don't ask her if she's fine, and she doesn't ask me either, which is all either of us can do for the other.

"You find her now," Gran says, voice breathy. I nod. She picks up her bowl of apples and goes back to peeling, and I try not to notice how much her hands shake.

"I'll check in with you as soon as I know something," I tell her.

Then I head for my truck.

The part of the county I live in is called Belfont, and it was never what you'd call rich. It was built up around a small coal mine, as a lot of places here in southwest Virginia used to be, and you can still see the bones of the old company store in amongst the leaves in the fall, right off the tracks. Gran grew up in the house Amey and I live in now, which was two rooms—one for cooking and bathing and supper, one for sleeping. Archie built onto it when he married in, a second son with no land of his own, one room at a time as he got up the money. There used to be an outhouse out back, before we used Amey's momma's money to fix the house up and put plumbing in. I was really little then, and Archie was still alive, so I don't remember what the house looked like before. But it's a homely thing now, sort of confused about if it's one story or two. We put white vinyl on it a few years ago to keep from having to paint it all the time, but the windows are still old and rattle in the wind in a storm, and the roof slopes nearly to the ground, making it seem hunched from the road. Still, it's ours.

I stare at the house longingly in my rearview mirror, wishing I was headed anywhere but where I'm going. The growing dark between the trees swallows it quickly.

When I was growing up, we were poor. Gran worked at the health clinic doing paperwork and the like. We got all of our vaccines there. Archie had worked at the munitions plant before he died, and they paid pretty good, so Gran and him had been well off when they raised my momma and Aunt May. But then May and her husband died, and then Archie followed them not long after. My momma ran off, and there we all were, Gran, Amey, and I, in a house that was five rooms and a bathroom, learning to live together on a little less than nothing. Without some government assistance, we'd have had problems. We didn't get much of what you'd call community support on account of not going to church. Gran has a good relationship with the Lord, but she doesn't much care for modern religious practices, or really any religion telling her she's fornicating with the Devil.

I thought of putting Randy's body underwater, but my creek isn't big enough to hold him under deep, and I don't talk to the river. The river doesn't belong to me, and I don't belong to it, and that's intentional on my part, no matter what the river thinks about it. We're in deep enough without me making bargains with an ancient body of water that stretches clear to Ohio. Rivers are dragons, make no mistake. They aren't cruel on purpose, but their concerns aren't your concerns, and you forget that to your peril.

So not to the river, then. I'd had some time to think on it, and that left an option I didn't much like, which was stowing the body far enough off the main roads that no one would likely find it until I could find Amey and get her to actually bury it deep.

Assuming she is alive. And if she isn't, well, Randy Higgins won't be the only murder charge I'll have to deal with. If Jack Higgins kills my cousin, I'll be sending him after her.

She must have touched earth, for the yard to spit Randy's body back up so suddenly. There's no way anyone could hold her if she were touching the earth now, but she'd been alive this afternoon, and somewhere on the mountain that rooted itself in my creek. The flowers and the creek thought so, too. Amey is alive, and if I want to keep myself out of jail and able to help her, I have to hide this dead man in the woods tonight and hope no one finds him. There's only one good place I can think of for that.

Trains come through this area like clockwork. You can follow the tracks all the way through the mountains, if you're brave or stupid. Unlike in the city, where the train tracks are fenced off, people can get on the tracks here anytime if they need to, though the rail companies still discourage it. The tracks run along the mountains on wide beds of thick gravel cut into their sides, connecting one far-flung town to another, and there's whole stretches where no one lives nearby. Sometimes couples come out here to neck, sometimes hunters use them to get places they technically aren't supposed to be. Tonight, my truck jumps and skitters over the rocks beside the tracks like it's got a guilty conscience, which it does. I'm driving it, after all.

I think of Randy's family. He has a girlfriend, and I'm pretty sure his mom is still alive. They're going to wonder where he got to. They're going to search. The sheriff will look high and low for family. It'll be on social media and in the paper. Eventually they'll grieve, but before that they will live in frantic, angry hope. That means I only have a few days to get this resolved, one way or another. Someone will think to talk to Jack eventually, and Amey needs to be back home acting normal before that happens.

I pull my truck as far off the gravel of the tracks as I can manage and turn off the engine. The truck door is heavy, and the old mechanism creaks as it swings open. I study the tree line in the headlights for a moment, then reach up to switch them off.

This part I'll need to do in the dark.

I only have another half hour before the next train, so I have to make this quick. There's no worry about Randy waking up undead on me, at least. Once Gran puts a spirit to rest, they stay that way. A few people still call her for it, if they're desperate enough. Cash from that bought more than one of my Christmas presents growing up.

I'm thankful for the muscles given to me by gardening and woodworking as I lift Randy's tarp-wrapped corpse down from the truck bed. There's no use trying to drag it through the brambles, so I sling the body across my shoulders as best I can and make my careful way into the woods. It's ponderous and my legs shake, but I can make it far enough before I have to put him down. The bigger issue is my gag reflex. He's been a few hours in that truck bed, and the day wasn't cool —Randy, the shell of him, stinks. It's not overwhelming yet, and it helps that the thick, creek-bottom mud is all over him, covering it up, but I can feel the smell burrowing its way into my sinuses. If I stop to think about how gross it is, I'm going to vomit. If I vomit, I'll drop this corpse and never be able to pick it up again out here in the darkness.

Woods at night are hard to navigate, no matter who you are, but the plants mostly keep to themselves when they sense me coming, so I only have to worry about unexpected dips in the earth to foil my steps. In ten minutes, I've worked myself far enough back in the woods that I feel confident the smell won't be overwhelming from the tracks, which is the best I can do. I sit the body down—it thumps more like I've thrown it and I wince even though I know Randy can't feel it—and try to ignore the muscle in my back jerking like a hooked fish as I pick my way back to the truck for a flashlight and a shovel.

It won't be long before the evening train comes. I have to hurry.

The first thing a witch does is learn to be unobtrusive. I stroke the side of my truck, smearing the dust that's accumulated on its green hide, and when my hand comes away, the truck's a little bit harder to see. It won't last long, so I hurry back under the trees with the shovel in my hands. I don't use the flashlight until I think I've come near where I set the body. I've put a red cover on it to save my night vision. It won't carry as far, but it gives everything an eerie glow. I catch the eyes of what is probably a raccoon in the tree nearby as I swing around, searching for the grey of the tarp. It's hard to see even with the light, but I find it. I pick a likely spot, one I can't sense many roots in, and push at the leaves and rocks until I hit thick loam. Then I dig down with the shovel. I feel the forest's attention focus on me. The night bugs go quieter, and I whisper an apology to the woods.

"Don't mean to disturb things, and you'll be glad of new bones," I tell it, softly, and the bug-song gets a bit louder as some of the pressure of watching lessens.

When I have a shallow pit about the length of a man, I drag Randy over next to it. There's a lot less brush to catch him this deep in the canopy, but it's still not easy, and I rip my tarp. I exhale a sigh. Wasn't like I would be able to use it again anyway, but I'd liked that tarp. I can never seem to find ones that aren't blue lately.

Then I brace myself and lift the edge. The leverage of the tarp does its work, and the body tumbles into the depression, limbs akimbo. I wince and try to do some rearranging, though my gut heaves. This is a horror show, red light and corpses and singing, sawing night bugs. With relief, I throw some dirt on the body from my digging, then cover it all over with rocks and leaves, obscuring the sight.

"I'd take kindly if you discouraged people from this particular spot for a few days," I tell the forest. Then I feed it just a little nudge of power, a payment. I can't tell a forest what to do, but it's alive, and I can ask nicely. The leaves shake on the trees, and Randy's body sinks a bit deeper into the earth, roots slithering over it. Even for me, it is unsettling.

I pick my way out of the woods on trembling legs. It is no hardship to crawl into the truck's cab, close the door to kill the light, and wait for the train. The tracks are already singing.

It blows through like a gale, clattering and shuddering over the tracks, but it doesn't sound its whistle. The conductor's eyes have slid off of me and the truck I've spelled, and when the bright lights of the engine are safely down the tracks, I start up and use the long body of the train to hide my return home.

CHAPTER THREE

THIS IS when you'd expect me to go haring off, probably. That's Amey's way of doing things—impassioned, urgent. But I am covered in mud and sweat, and I last ate at about one in the afternoon. There's been a lot of heavy lifting between now and then, and I'm dead on my feet. Plus, Amey's chickens need feeding, if something hasn't already gotten into the unlocked coop and killed them all.

More importantly, I don't have a plan. I know Jack by reputation, mostly, the way everybody in a small community knows everybody else. He lives in Belfont, but up the mountain. There are a lot of scattered houses up there, once you get past the church and the fire station. Maybe if I were part of the congregation I would know more, but that particular church is the hellfire and brimstone kind. I wouldn't be welcome.

Jack isn't much for church either. He has a wife, named Marie, and the both of them are frequent customers at the bar. Spike's is back in town, in Mattock proper. The place offers generally terrible food, including favorites such as mozzarella sticks and overcooked burgers. Really they just have food on the menu as an excuse to serve drinks and to catch the Sunday lunch crowd. It's where Amey works while she's in school getting her Associate's at the community college. Amey wants to be a nurse—she says it pays well enough, she might could even afford her own place one day. I don't know how I feel about her leaving, but it's not like she can go far, and I'd like to see her get out of that bar. Lots of rough folks hang out there Saturday night—like Jack.

So instead of rushing out to do who-knows-what, I drive myself home.

The house is dark, and I go through and flip on every light, feeling my nerves twitch. I rummage through the cupboard, pull out a can of ravioli, crack it open, and dump it into a bowl in the microwave. Go to the phone on the wall—cell phones don't work between the mountains like we are, so we still have a landline—and call Gran. She answers.

Normally, we chat about our days, but for a moment, I can't think of what words to say.

"I put away the chickens," Gran says.

I open my mouth to admonish her—I know how tired she was after sending Randy on—but I sigh instead and settle on thanks. I'm too tired to think straight, the long day finally catching up to me. I'll rally with food, but the chickens don't deserve my inadequacy.

"You going to try scrying?" Calm, like she's talking about the weather, but we both know that I don't scry for just anything. It opens you up to the world too much.

"Yeah," I say, and don't say that I can't think of what else to do.

Every witch has her strengths. Amey is a powerful witch who killed a man with nothing but bare earth and chicken blood, but I'm not like her. Even if I had dumped Randy's body in the river, I couldn't have been sure the river would keep him. The creek and I do well together, but the creek can't make a river behave, and as I've mentioned, the river does what it wants. I don't have too much sway with water, despite it being my element. I can tweak the weather when we need it and find a well if you ask. Otherwise, my power is not that kind.

No, I'm a diviner, like Archie. I take a deep breath. The microwave pings.

"Good luck, Rhia," Gran says to me.

I nod, though she can't see. Then I clear my throat.

"Goodnight, Gran," I say.

~

This kind of divination is simple enough. First, I fill a bowl with water. I could probably use any bowl, but I use a plain steel mixing bowl that reminds me of the silver they used to back mirrors with. Steel isn't a normal medium; Archie taught me on crystal, but that bowl was his, and it doesn't really like me. I still keep it in the cupboard. I have a copper bowl for spellwork, when I deign to do it, a gift from Amey.

I could probably use any water. Archie could, but every witch is a little bit different. To be safe, I always use water from the creek, which now necessitates walking down the backyard in the dead of night. The moon is a waning sliver in the sky above my head, and I shudder as I pass by the spot where Randy died. The night bugs are still singing, and the shadows of bats flit across the sky. The creek, tense and sleeping, is cold with the coming fall.

Once I'm back up to the kitchen, I light a candle. The candle is beeswax, a tapered thing I got from the market, and it makes the whole room smell sweet. Rosemary Blankenship sells them in the fall after she has harvested her hives. She's one of the few neighbors on this mountain I get along with, probably because anyone the bees have decided to like can't be all bad.

I pop my candle into a wine bottle I have kept just for this purpose, its neck already coated with wax, and turn the lights off in the kitchen. The fire isn't necessary, but it gives me something to focus on. In the dark, it reflects on the water's surface, dancing. If I unfocus my eyes, and breathe real slow, and don't think about anything . . .

I'm somewhere dark, and that is normal until I realize the candle's light is gone and someone is crying.

"Shush, baby," comes Amey's voice. It's rough, and I know it's because she's been screaming. The knowing should bother me, but the vision is a glimmer on the water, and I am underneath.

"It's going to be alright." She's lying. She doesn't know if it's going to be alright. She can't touch the earth—nothing but wood and dead concrete under her feet. If Rhia were here—

I feel her reach into the vision then. It's like when we were children, and she slept beside me in our small bed. She turns, and she whispers.

"Rhia? Is that you?"

I can't find words in the dream, but she doesn't need them. "Rhia, there's not much time. Jack's got us—" an impression of pain, an ache in her head, the jumbling of a long, half-conscious ride up the mountain. "He knows. I didn't mean to, Rhia. You have to hurry."

My heart clenches. I open my mouth, to say what I don't know, but that's a mistake, I know better—

The vision shatters.

I'm back in the kitchen, my head ringing with the aftermath of looking so far. For a moment, I just sit there, mouth dry, and let the world spin around me. The ever-present sound of the creek comes through the open windows, and the crying of the night bugs, and my head is as blank and empty as the dark of the room.

Jack doesn't just know. Jack took her. He hurt her; I can still feel the phantom bruises as if they were my own. He's mean, Jack, but he is probably panicking now—trying to figure through his options. Kidnapping is a crime, and if he lets Amey go, she'll kill him if she can, or at least he has no reason to think she won't. I wouldn't have said Jack was dumb enough to make himself a killer, but all men can be killers in the right circumstances, and he's already closer to it than most.

What will he do with her? And who was she talking to, in the darkness?

My hands shake as I reach for the candle and snuff it out.

~

It's funny that Amey is considered the normal of the two of us, because she is the most hot-headed witch I know. Gran says it's the earth in her, always trying to make her still, bumping up against her stubbornness. A tectonic interaction, the kind that shatters cities. She can't stand to play by the rules, which I guess is more normal in this day and age than being a duty-bound older sibling in a broken family. I kept to myself, studied, helped Gran with the bills when I could, though it's hard for a little girl to convince anyone to pay her to mow their yard. I took to carving early because I liked the stability of it, the peacefulness of sitting by the creek and letting my knife move through the wood. When I was still doing little things—before I had graduated into carpentry and the like—Gran sold my trinkets by word of mouth. People seemed to think they were good luck. Maybe they were.

Amey, by contrast, was an outgoing, slender little firecracker of a girl, with red hair and freckles and a smile as wide as it was bright. Gran let her sign up for soccer, and that was that—she was off like a rocket. Amey ran and jumped and danced and laughed at the right times. That laugh was infectious. You heard it, and you fell in love. She broke her first heart when she was thirteen and never looked back.

The key to the mess we've found ourselves in is that there is someone else in that place with her. I've got to figure out who. I remember a sense of concrete, of stale and still air. I barely sleep at all, and my dreams are of that place, of the absolute lightlessness, of the stiff scents of fear and sweat and blood.

When dawn comes, I am already awake, brewing.

A water witch is a witch with certain predilections. Water is the base of every living thing. Man was made from clay, but it takes water to work it. I see visions, which is a slightly separate thing, and certainly not exclusive to being called to the water. Fire witches can do it sometimes, which may be why my visions are so strong. Mom was always best with fire, I'm told. In any case, it's not my only skill, just the one I'm most easy with.

So, first thing in the morning, I climb out of bed. My bedroom is on the east side, and it gets good light, but though a few birds are trying to decide whether to wake up or not, it's still dark. The predawn air coming through my window is damp and cold with fall's early chill. I pace on bare feet across the cold wood of the floor to the bookshelf by my bed, and pull loose a large binder, the kind folks keep recipes in. Then I carry it downstairs into the kitchen. The old floor in the hallway creaks and pops under the thin carpet. I do not look at Amey's closed door as I pass by.

The fancy books the Wiccan kids buy at the store call what I've got in my hands a Book of Shadows. That's always seemed a might ostentatious as far as titles go. I call it my recipe book. I copied the things in it from Gran's collection, who copied it from her Ma before, and I add to it sometimes when I need to. Knowing how to read and write used to be far more unusual than it is now, and we all got in the habit of keeping our notes away from prying eyes. As Gran used to say, the Bible is for company, but your book is private. Not that Amey or I are much inclined to keep a Bible out—or to have much company for that matter. I think Amey would be more social but for me. We have people up every now and again, but I've been so isolated it feels like putting on a stranger's skin to entertain. Selling things to folks on Wednesday and Saturday is fine, but there's no call to go and get personal.

The kitchen is quiet. I leave my book on the table, with the candle from the night before and the creek water in its bowl. The vision is still heavy in my stomach. I stare at the empty water, thinking for a moment that it might reveal more to me.

It doesn't. The power in this water is spent. I pick up the steel bowl, get my copper bowl down too, and carry them both outside. There are things to be doing, and not a lot of time to be doing them.

There's mist settled over everything, and my boots clomp down the porch stairs. I cast a glance around the yard, eying the turned-up place Randy came out of like it might pop out some other gift. It's still a muddy mess, though at least the blood and feathers are gone.

I stamp over to the chicken coop and let the hens out. They're hesitant to emerge, which makes sense—we all had a rough day yesterday, and I'm not Amey. Plus, it's pretty early still. I leave them to figure it out, scattering some feed for them to find when they get over their fright, and take my bowls to the creek. I dump the old water out of my steel bowl and fill the copper one to the brim. Then I head back to the house.

The book is waiting.

I haven't eaten, but my stomach is uninterested, and I can't force myself to it. Amey makes me eat when I get like this, but Amey isn't here. I allow the vision to creep back into me, the hard concrete of the floor, the sound of crying.

Jack has her, and that means I need to go get her. I know Jack's house is up on the mountain, and I know it was Marie's parents' place. Marie is his wife, married him right out of high school before she wised up to his bullshit. She's always struck me as a nice enough woman, but would she try to help Amey? I've never talked to her much, though I know she's one of the regulars at Spike's. That's more riding on Jack's coattails than anything else. I stay away from that place. Smells too much like liquor, which is failure and guilt and not a lot else for me, but if this keeps up, I guess I'll be going to visit Bobbie, the proprietor. I doubt he's fired Amey yet—she's good-looking, and Bobbie is a distant relation on Archie's side somewhere, not that that always means much.

Jack might expect me to be looking for her, though, and once I start, I will be calling attention to the whole thing. We don't need attention. There's a dead man needs to stay buried. And attention might push Jack toward action, and desperate men turn monster fast, even when they start out kind. Jack's not kind. He's been in trouble with the law before, and this situation is the kind that puts someone in jail. He will want to make it all go away. If I go turning over rocks, will he move up his plans?

I breathe, remind myself not to borrow trouble. Then I crack open my binder on the antique metal table to a well-worn page. Metal's good to work on, doesn't soak up moisture like wood does. My magic soaks into wood too quick. Before I start hunting, before I go to get Amey from wherever Jack is keeping her, I need backup. I need the only spells I can make.

The bowl of creek water waits for me.

I use glass measuring containers, and my will for stirring. The kitchen is large enough that I can spread out a little—the kitchen was the heart of the house when this one was built, back before things like microwaves or even electric ovens. It's not a frilly house, but it's solid, and the kitchen remains its heart still. The cabinets are old, hand-hung things painted white, and an old icebox still sits propped in the corner. I use it for herbs now. I pop the iron latch, and the smell of dried plants floods the room. I prefer to work with living things, or at least green ones, but there's not enough time to collect what I need.

Inside the cabinet are bags and bundles, mushrooms and roots and bits of bark, leaves ground and whole, berries shriveled and tinctured. I weigh spells in my head. There's one for strength—I doubt I'll sleep again, or get much time for eating, and I'll possibly need to take a punch. Endurance is its own magic. I haven't brewed that up since Amey played soccer. We both agreed it wasn't really cheating, even if we knew we were lying. I pull out burdock root and moonshine from Sam's still, a man I know for a fact takes care with his distilling. Add a few more easily acquired herbs like rosemary. There's nothing in the potion I'm making that can't be found or grown around here, and nothing that would really hurt or help a body without a witch's touch to give it a bit more of a kick. That's the secret to all potions, to every bit of kitchen alchemy you can find. It's a knack, nothing more. Nothing less either.

It takes time to break up my ingredients. I use a mortar—it's stone, an item kept exclusively for spellwork. I mix and stir and push my will into it, thinking of being fast, being strong. Thinking of feeling no pain. It's meditative, and the creek is whispering in my head as I sprinkle moonshine and clear water into my mixture. My head is humming with the sound of water, a continuous outward breath to the sea I have never seen.

My fingers gather up a bit of the resulting paste, spread it on my lips. It is bitter and herbal and earthy all at once, and the magic peaks in me like the sun catching a stream in the morning, bright and hopeful. I know it's done then, and exhale deeply, scooping the slurry of it into a small glass jar. It will last me a day at least, three at most.

I flip forward in the book, looking for something else useful. There are poisons in the back, and I'm considering the possibilities when I hear gravel crunch from the front of the house.

Who is here?

I'm already packing up my things, especially the recipe book, jogging it back to my room as quickly as I can. The paste is in its jar, and I move it to the counter where it won't be so obvious, and stick the mortar in the sink to be cleaned. The herbs go in the icebox, and I'm left with one odd copper bowl of creek water. I could dump it down the sink, but the creek doesn't like it when I do that, even if it all ends up in the yard eventually anyway. The septic field is a sore point between the creek and myself, even though I'm not the one responsible for putting it in. That would be Archie. It beats a straight pipe, anyway. And both Amey and I are adamant that an outhouse is a nonstarter.

There's a knock at the door. They've come to the back door, so it must be someone I've told to do that, and I can't for the life of me think of who it would be. I consider pretending not to be home, think of my truck, think of Randy's body in the truck last night, and the guilt of burying him. All of this seemed manageable just a few moments ago, and now I realize I'm going to have to talk to another human being as if the last day hasn't happened at all.

It hits me then who must be at the door. My hand is on the doorknob before I've made a conscious decision to cross to it.

He's facing away from me when the door swings open, about to walk down the porch steps. At the sound, he turns. His eyes light up, warm and brown.

"Hey, Rhia," he says. "I thought maybe you were out to church."

I force a smile, and surprise myself when it comes easily.

"Owen," I say in greeting. I step outside and close the door. "I did tell you to come by."

I had, too. I could kick myself.

Owen is a tall drink of water, well-muscled, with tight, curly hair that shades to gold on the ends and a scruff of beard. You can tell he's always been beautiful, but somehow that beauty hasn't spoiled him. Don't ask me how, because aside from Amey, I have not before now had good experiences with beautiful people. The muscle that makes me look stocky and overlarge makes him look sculpted and lean, which is a neat trick as these things go. Mine comes from gardening and home maintenance and carpentry. His probably comes from the gym. There's one in town, though I've never been.

I finished Owen's table last week, but he couldn't come to the farmer's market and pick it up yesterday, so we arranged for him to pick it up today. I'd had some idea, when I'd given him my address, that maybe I would make him lunch, or at least offer him coffee—something casual, some excuse to spend more time. He's a foolish thing to dream of, Owen, too pretty by half and educated besides. He's moved back out here to take care of his parents, who are in poor health, but he travels often enough for work. Does something with computers, I think, though I don't really know enough about him to say what.

"Is now a bad time?" He has such a crisp accent. Could never tell he grew up around here. Then again, both of his parents were educated, and he went out of state for school—New York or somewhere, I really can't remember with him looking at me like that. I realize I need to say something, so I make my mouth move.

"Kind of, yeah," I say. And then my mouth decides to keep moving, and I tell him, "Amey's gone missing."

I can see the change come over him, from concern to honest-to-God worry, and I throw up my hands in defense. Of all the things to say. I try to backpedal.

"I'm sorry, I'm sorry, it's probably nothing, but she wasn't home when I got back yesterday, and I was worried, and she's still not back." I'm babbling. The self-deprecation sounds honest, even if I normally wouldn't bother with it. My stomach is doing a little squirm of revulsion, and I can't decide if it's for lying or for kowtowing.

"I forgot you were coming," I finish lamely.

"Rhia—" he begins. My heart stutters in panic.

"Come on, I'll show you my workshop," I say, but he puts his hand on my shoulder when I try to push past him. The shock of that contact sets me still as stone, though his touch is gentle.

"Rhia, hold on. Have you called anyone about this?"

I grit my teeth. This is why a girl shouldn't run her fool mouth. "I'm sure she'll turn up," I say. "I don't want to make a big deal over nothing."

I can see him struggle to swallow that, but he doesn't press the issue. It raises my opinion of him, and I do not need that right now.

"But you're here for a table," I say, pushing free of his hand. "Come on, this way."

The workshop is actually toward the front of the house, in the side yard off the gravel driveway, so I can load things easily. The backyard is solidly in the floodplain, and the tools I use for my work are too big of an investment to risk drowning them because the creek is having a bad week. I built it mostly by hand in the months after dropping out of college. It kept me from going crazy, and it was a good use of the student loan money I didn't need anymore. Gotta love those expensive books. And I had been in engineering, so they had been plenty expensive.

Owen follows me down the stairs and around the house, to the garage I've built on the other side of the circular drive. I've got a padlock on the door, but it's not actually locked, more there for show, and I slide it out of the door handle and turn it sharply up. The hum of a dehumidifier greets my ears, and the smell of wood makes something inside me unclench.

The man steps in behind me, bringing his aftershave and male smell into the workshop space. I don't know what he expects, but he makes a sound of surprise.

"It looks bigger on the inside," he says.

"It's the windows." The light is a good aid when I'm trying to work on details, and staring at the creek can be soothing when I need inspiration. I put windows all down one wall, and this early in the day, the sun is just starting to peek over the trees and highlight the whole workshop.

I built it mostly through careful planning and a lot of patience. I'd built the deck before, and so I understood the basics of measuring and cutting and aligning, sanding and finishing. The garage, which is really just a glorified shed on steroids, was a lot harder than the deck. It is all wood, except where it is glass, with siding on the outside to insulate and keep out the elements. It had taken all of my attention and skill. For a moment, the feeling of well-being I always get when I come to the workshop floods me.

Then I remember Amey, and the feeling fades.

"Did you build this yourself? How long did it take you?" Owen has passed me by in my reverie and is inspecting the walls hung with tools. I like that he doesn't touch anything.

I'm proud of my shed, so having Owen in it makes my stomach knot up, for all his good manners. He's so clean cut and educated with his fine degrees and his white collar job, and I'm just a college dropout who makes things with my hands. Yes, they're useful things, but they're small—decks, tables, keychains, stools. There's every chance someone like him could look down on someone like me. But he steps around the workshop and studies the walls with focus. Some of the tools he looks at are old hand-me-downs scavenged from Archie's things or yard sales. Some are new acquisitions. I make enough that occasionally there's some left over from my part of the bills, and it's not like I spend it on fancy dresses. No, I'm a power tools kind of girl these days.

"You use all these?" Owen asks. He doesn't wait for an answer. "My dad taught me basic home repair and the like, but I've never seen some of these tools."

"Maybe I can teach you sometime," I say, trying for lighthearted and not strangled-with-nerves. He casts me a grin that makes my heart stagger in my chest, then turns at last to look at the reason we're both here.

The table is a special order on his part. Unlike most of my products, it's not an entirely original piece. Before I got a touch carried away, it was a pretty basic refurbishment. I've been tying myself in knots about it for weeks, much to Amey's amusement, worried I'd taken things a little too far but unable to quite stop myself. I don't do refurbishments often, and there's a reason. The wood wants what it wants, and it's not in me to ignore that.

This particular table was his great-grandmother's on his mother's side, a long dining room piece that had been in storage since her death several decades ago. She'd taken care of him when he was little, lived with him and his parents until she died of old age. That's how families are out here, intertwined like that, even well-off families like his sometimes. His own mother, Mrs. Moore, had been raised by her grandmother, much like me, though in her case, her mother had died. More like Amey, I guess. In any case, she'd loved the old walnut table, and when water had gotten into the storage shed and caused the clear varnish to bubble and the legs to warp and crack, she'd given it up for lost. Owen, though, had decided to see if it was salvageable.

I have salvaged it, but it doesn't look much like it did before. The dark wood still shines under a clear varnish, sure, but after I'd sanded the old varnish off, I etched a design in the tabletop, pulling the eye away from any remaining imperfections, before coating it again. And the legs aren't straight, spindly things anymore, but a sensuous curve of limbs carved from my own scavenged stores of walnut wood. I debated long and hard over parting with them, but the table needed it. Overall, it's a very different piece of furniture, and I've held my breath for as long as I can in the silence.

"What do you think?" I ask. Owen is tracing the designs with his fingers, and he rests his palm on the tabletop when he hears my voice.

"It's beautiful." He says it quietly. His hand brushes the new varnish again, and I feel something unlock inside me.

"I can tell it's the same table," he says, "it just feels familiar. But it's so different. How did you do that?"

He doesn't seem to expect an answer, but I give one anyway.

"Wood just talks, I guess." It's an admission I wouldn't make to just anyone. Seems I'm full of those, with him. I clear my throat.

"Let's get it in your truck."

All that old wood is heavy, and it takes both of us to load the thing into Owen's lined truck bed. I did most of the work in pieces, assembling it as I went, even knowing that meant a risk if things didn't line up just so. I haven't tried to move the fully assembled table by myself, and as we haul it to the truck, I thank my lucky stars for my own good sense. That's part of why I asked Owen to come pick it up himself—even with two of us, it's a near thing getting it loaded without dropping it or knocking it on something.

Still, we manage, and Owen wraps it carefully in blankets and straps it down to keep it steady, then jumps back down from his truck bed. I'm stretching my back, which is sore from my evening adventures. I straighten when Owen comes around the truck, checkbook in hand. He rips the check clear and hands it to me.

"This is more than we agreed on," I say, looking at the paper in my hands. My voice is high with surprise. There's an extra digit on this number. I shove it back towards him. He steps out of reach.

"You didn't just refinish it," he says. "I know you made those legs from nothing. That's a work of art, Rhia. Don't sell yourself short."

It takes me a minute to put words in my mouth. He's not wrong, but he didn't ask for me to do that, and how can you just decide to give someone that much more money on a whim? How rich do you have to be? I almost ask, but that would be rude as all hell, so I bite my tongue, grasping at words, and lose valuable moments. He's already closed himself in his truck.

"But it's not what we agreed on," I manage. I jog up to the window. "I don't want charity, Owen."

I've shoved the check under his nose. He sighs and turns off the engine.

"Take it, Rhia. You deserve every penny of it. I won't feel right if I pay you less."

"And I won't feel right if I take it," I say, unmoving.

He grimaces, but he reaches for his checkbook again. Writes a new number, back in the three-digit range but still a lot more than what I'd asked for.

"Compromise?" he says.

It's my turn to grimace, my mouth twisting, but I take it. We'll need the extra money with Amey missing shifts, and he's right. I should be charging more, except the people around here can't pay that much normally, and I've been putting off selling to the rich folks in the cities. They'll write those four- and five-figured checks without thinking about it.

"I didn't mean to insult you, Rhia," he says, voice low and smooth as butter. I know it's the truth, too. I run my hands through my hair, wishing I could be mad. It would be easier to let all this tension out at somebody.

"I believe you," I say, then swallow. "Let me know what your mom thinks."

He smiles, eyes lighting up. "I will," he says. Then, "If you don't hear from Amey . . ." He breaks off, searching my face. I realize I've gone as tense as a board. I see the moment he decides to drop it, to switch tactics. "Just let me know if you need anything, Rhia."

There's so much intensity in his gaze that I swallow, feeling my heart bounce and tumble. He's beautiful and good.

And I'm halfway to being a murderer.

"Thanks," I say, soft as heartbreak.

Then I step back and let him go.

CHAPTER FOUR

OWEN IS GONE, but my heart is too unsettled for spellwork. I have questions and Amey has a job we can't afford for her to lose. I head for the bar.

It's early, so Spike's isn't open yet. My truck rumbles its way into the parking lot, spitting and growling. I need to clean the spark plugs. Thinking about that keeps me from thinking about the empty truck bed, which I sprayed out last night for good measure.

Mattock is a quiet town on a Sunday morning. It's late enough the air has lost the new blush of dawn, and that reveals the town's imperfections. The courthouse and the long rail park look cared for, of course, but the private buildings are a different story. Some, like the churches, are pristine. Most of the shopfronts are boarded up. A few, like my friend Gerry's Mustard Seed Cafe, show the signs of fledgling investment.

Spike's is on the outer edge of downtown proper, just a few lots up from the parking lot where the farmer's market sets up. Where most of the buildings are old brick, pressed tight to the road, Spike's is newer, set back behind a vacant, potholed parking lot. Without cars, it feels barren, exposed. The road is empty but for my truck. This early everyone is either in church or sleeping off their Saturday night.

Rightly, you wouldn't think a bar would open on a Sunday, but Spike's also doubles as one of Mattock's only lunch spots. Since they don't do Sunday brunch like the Mustard Seed, they open at 11:30, which means I've got a half hour before Amey is late for her ten o'clock opening shift. Bobbie always gets in early, though. Sundays are good days for paperwork, he says. Nobody calls a bar on Sunday morning. There's not likely to be anyone around to notice my visit, at least.

I park my truck, turn off the ignition, and flip down the visor. Tired eyes stare back at me from the mirror.

"Why the hell did you have to run your mouth?" I ask myself. It was stupid to say anything to Owen. It's probably stupid to come here. Amey may be missing, but so is Randy Higgins, even if no one knows it yet. It was self-defense, but that won't make any difference, especially since I will be an accessory to murder, but damnit, what was I supposed to do?

"Just breathe, Rhia." Talking to myself is something I do when the world is hard, which is more days than I like to admit, but answering myself? That's reserved for special occasions. I follow my own advice, inhaling and exhaling, feeling the creek running in the back of my mind all cool and steady. Then I pop open the door and cross the parking lot.

There's a delivery entrance, and it has a doorbell. I circle around and press the button. There's a chime inside, something generic, and then I stand there fidgeting and casting surreptitious glances up Main Street, waiting. The church parking lot is full, cars gleaming in the sun before it slides behind a cloud, and I'm sweating a bit before Bobbie comes to the door.

"Rhia," he says, looking surprised, then concerned. "What are you doing here?"

"Bobbie." I pause, working words around. "Amey sent me." Lie. "She's not feeling well." Not exactly a lie, but close enough that it makes me squirm a little. Bobbie senses my discomfort.

"Is this about Marie?"

I blinked. What does Amey being sick have to do with Jack's wife?

"Oh, don't give me that look," Bobbie says. "I've known there was something between them for a while. Always talking together when it's slow. Obviously Marie wasn't interested because she spent Friday night screaming at Amey in the bathroom before she stormed out of here. Right before close, luckily, because Amey wasn't worth shit after that. Sent her home early."

He eyes me, taking in my shocked look.

"She tell you she was sick? Tell her to get over it. Messing around with Old Jack's girl—that's stupidity, and she ain't stupid. You get on home and tell her that. If she's not back on Wednesday, she can stay gone. I ain't got use for someone that dumb."

"Bobbie—" I start, but he's closed the door in my face. I'm as shocked by the rudeness as anything, but my mind catches up as I'm reaching to ring the doorbell again.

Messing around with Marie? Amey?

"Fuck," I say, and drop my hand. I head back to my truck, then change direction. I need coffee, and breakfast. I've been up for a few hours now, and my head has gone light. There's one other person who might know what's going on, who will be able to put this picture together in my head. One person Amey might have confided in if she wasn't confiding in me. I head to the Mustard Seed.

The Mustard Seed Cafe is a block down from the bar and around the corner, next to an abandoned department store. Mattock used to be a nice place. The buildings have good bones. It's years of financial turmoil and disinvestment, delayed care and falling populations that have left it looking this way. Some of us try to change that as we can. The farmer's market and the new cafe have caught on well enough to stay afloat for now. There's biking and hiking trails nearby, so we get some tourists. There are lots of reasons for folks to look down on places like this, and I agree with some of them. But when I'm not too run down, I can see what it could be. Today, I just see the closed storefronts and Bobbie's viperous words.

Food will help, but I can't help feeling guilty I'm stopping at all. Is Amey getting food right now?

The bell on the door to the cafe tinkles as I press through. I force myself to stop and study the repurposed church pews, the overstuffed couch, the watercolors on the walls. It's a cozy little place. I walk up to the bar—I carved it, and every time I see it, calm floods me at the smooth driftwood lines of it, the red and gold striations of the wood. It was an absolutely ancient cherry that fell in Gerry's yard one summer—luckily missing her garden—and I'd made good on several of the pieces I'd hauled home when she called me, so I'd done the bar for her for free. Amey had yelled at me for a week when she found out.

Amey—what am I doing? Whatever Gerry tells me doesn't change that I need to go after her. I should go home, finish my spellwork, and charge up the mountain to find her. But my legs stay rooted. I'm not bright and brave. When it matters, I fail.

Gerry's in the back somewhere—I can hear her humming a Fleetwood Mac song. When she emerges, drawn by the sound of the bell, her dark brown curls drawn up on her head and her long blue skirt swishing on her hips, I have to bite my tongue. The urge to tell her everything is as bright as blood in my mouth, and I realize I've come to do just that. I want someone to save me from this, to take the burden away.

"Rhia! I've missed you!" Gerry sashays around the bar like a dancer, which she is when we can make it out to the bar for the Thursday night fiddling session once a month. She's a few years older than me, with curly black hair and a tendency to wear bright colors that show off her olive skin. My heart should leap to see her, but it clenches instead.

Gerry doesn't need my shit. She has kids, and the shop, and she and her husband work hard to keep a roof over their heads. I have my secrets. But it's too late to leave now. I let her hug me, though not tightly. I don't want to have to explain myself when I fall apart. She kisses my cheeks, a habit from growing up in a Latino community out west, though she only does it with family. There's family you grow with, and family you adopt. Coming here was hard for Gerry, following her husband back to his family's land and leaving hers, and I'm not sorry to have been the person who got to be her shelter in that. I want to put my head on her shoulder, to return her openness with my own. I step back instead.

"What are you doing in town?" Gerry asks. I don't come in on Sundays usually, and certainly not this early. I force a smile.

"Amey's sick and you know how bad I cook," I say. Wonder what Gerry would think of me if Amey turned up dead tomorrow, if she knew how I'd spent my night, if she knew—nip that in the bud, because there's nowhere worth going down that road, and Gerry's already looking at me worried.

"Well, that's the truth," Gerry says, laughing. Then she sobers. "I heard she and Marie got into it Friday night. Is she okay?"

I blink, shocked a second time. Then the shock transforms.

"Am I the only one in town who didn't know Amey was sweet on Marie?" I demand.

Gerry looks bemused.

"Probably not, honey, but you're not the only one comes in here with your problems."

"Damnit," I say, feeling the need to throw something, feeling the itch to drown that need in anything. Back Creek comes welling up in my head, and I close my eyes and fall back into the cool flow of water, only to find that the water isn't enough. Amey hid this from me. She lied. The betrayal pushes me under. Water comes up around my chest, my neck, the pressing torrent of the flood.

And beneath the creek's familiar waters, there's a deeper flow, a growling of rocks caught in the current, a coughing roar—a gaze turning my direction. My eyes pop open in panic. I pull away from the water like it burns.

It's been a long time since the creek wasn't enough. My stomach flips and twists.

"Rhia, honey, you okay?" Gerry's voice has gone high and tight. She hates cursing as a rule, and at first I think that's all that's got her hackles up, but then I feel the sweat on my skin. I must be white as a sheet.

"Yea—" I say, the lie catching in my throat. I try again. "Yeah, I'm sorry, I just—uh, haven't had breakfast yet, feeling dizzy for some reason, you know." Babbling again. Hiding again. Who wouldn't see through that?

But Gerry seems to calm a little, and she lets me order food. I sit at the counter because I can't see any way to get out of it and because I'm not quite ready to face that I am scared of Jack. How am I going to get in there, find Amey, and get her out? I'm not James Bond. I'm not even the Scooby Gang. I'm just little old me, a broken girl held together by water.

I'm a couple of bites into biscuits and gravy and a fried egg with salsa, all from scratch, when Gerry says, "I didn't mean to hit you with that stuff about Amey."

I swallow, take a swig of coffee, black and hot to scald my tongue.

"Bobbie laid into me first thing this morning. I didn't even know her and Marie were . . . whatever they are. She didn't tell me." I don't mean to sound so hurt on that last, but there it is. She didn't tell me she was interested in someone, but then again, Amey and I haven't really been close since I went off to college, for all that we lived together. The competing schedules are part of it—I need the early mornings to work, and Amey is a night owl—but that isn't everything.

I've never told her everything.

"I heard they fought," Gerry said. "Everyone heard. Is she okay?"

"She's fine," I say. It's a half-hearted answer. Things are finally clicking into place. Amey and Marie fought—everyone saw and realized Amey was sweet on Marie. But that wasn't enough for Jack to do what he did, unless—

"Was Amey sleeping with Marie?" I hiss at Gerry. My friend looks guilty. I drop my fork and put my head in my hands. "Goddamnit." How did they even manage it? Everyone knows Jack's a controlling asshole. Unless—Amey had started leaving early for her shifts sometimes, saying she wanted to do some errands, and I hadn't thought anything of it. Jack keeps Marie on a tight leash, but it's not like he never lets her go anywhere at all. She still has work, times that are her own.

"Rhia, I'm sorry—"

I wave the apology off, feeling guilty already. None of this is Gerry's fault. It's not Amey's fault, or Marie's, either. It's just a mess all around.

"I've got to go, Gerry." I stand up. Breakfast is no longer something I can stomach. "Can I get my food boxed up?"

"Rhia," Gerry protests. She looks scared now. I've scared Gerry. I grit my teeth. "Rhia, what's wrong?"

"Gerry," I say, summoning every shred of earnestness I can muster, "this ain't your fault. But I may need you to look after the chickens for a while. I'm—We may not be around much."

She goes pale, flush leaving her brown skin. I don't know what I look like or what she's reading on my face, but whatever it is I know she won't leave it. I've said too much, implied too much, because I can't keep my fool mouth shut. I'm glad when I hear the bell ring behind me. A couple I don't know walks in wearing hiking clothes covered in the university logo.

"You'll call me." It isn't a question, but I don't meet Gerry's eyes. "Rhia, look at me."

I look, meet her brown eyes with mine. She's so fierce in this moment, like she can fight off anything. I want to tell her. I wasn't made for secrets, not this kind.

"Don't ask me, Gerry," I say instead.

She boxes up breakfast, and I go.

~

It's a long drive back to the house. Long enough for the fear, paralyzing thing, to get swallowed up in a knot of anger that will finally let me do what I need to do. It's time to finish my spellwork.

Jack's wife, Marie, is beautiful in a quiet way. Not the kind of woman you would think would be with someone like Jack. She looks sensible, but maybe that's the point—he wiggled his way into her head and dragged her down into the dark, and maybe that gives him more pleasure than anything.

Marie has tight platinum curls, and she wears them in a braid. She teaches at the middle school, and she's short, but round instead of stocky like me. She likes to read, I think, because a lot of times you'll see her car parked outside the library in the afternoons before she heads home up the mountain. That's about all I know about her beyond the fact that she was foolish enough to fall for Jack. That's not her fault, really. Monsters are just as like to use honey to bait their traps as anything else.

I know, now, who that other voice was, in the dark. And I can guess at where, too. Jack is mean, not imaginative. He'll have taken Amey to where he feels he has the most power. That house on the mountain is isolated. The question is what he plans to do with her.

I have to go to her. But I'm not a fighter. My best bet is to sneak in.

I study the materials I've pulled out, thinking about what can be used against a man as bitter-mean as Jack. Everyone's seen Marie's bruises. He won't have a problem hitting me, or worse, any more than he had a problem hitting Marie or Amey.

So what then? I know spells for healing, for banishing spirits and ill luck, for calling the same down onto someone's head. I know spells for lust and stamina, for bringing love, for babies and for good crops. I've used nearly every one of them for Gran or Amey's friends, or occasionally for myself. None of them will work to stop a man with a gun.

There's only one thing I think might be useful. It's not a potion, exactly. There's still enough water in the bowl to do it, so I reach for the creek, hearing its murmured welcome. Tasting the edge of trouble on the water's surface, like a skim of bitter oil.

I think, in that moment, that I don't need the warning. Whatever can go wrong has already gone and done it. I'm right, but not the way I think I am.

The creek water has gone coppery from the bowl. It slides into my mouth, metal and cool, musty earth on my tongue. I purse my lips around the bare mouthful of it, like I'm playing a flute, which I did, briefly, in middle school. Not my instrument, the flute, but I had the right mouth shape for it, and that means a lot when you're young and getting pushed at extracurriculars. I blow air out, slow and gentle, letting it pass over the water in my mouth. Willing it to become something else.

It does. Vapor seeps past my lips, forms a white cloud in front of my face, though the air isn't cold. It's a long exhale, and I'm nearly seeing stars by the time I've marshaled all the water into the form I want it to be in.

Quickly, I pop the cap off three more vials. They're test tubes with little plastic lids—cheap special orders from the internet. The cloud goes into the vials. If I had to describe the creek's feelings on taking water, I'd normally use the word peevish. It doesn't like it when I take water and don't put it back. But the creek seems less concerned today. Maybe it knows this isn't just me playing a prank on a neighbor. This is serious.

The test tubes capped, I slide them into my jeans next to my truck keys, grateful for my large pockets. Amey gives me shit for not being fashionable sometimes, but there's nothing that beats a good, thick pair of jeans with pockets. None of that stretchy stuff she likes for me.

It's getting chilly outside, a sudden wind ushering fall's chill into the summer afternoon, so I grab a jacket before I go see to the work that needs to be done about the house. The herbs and the book need to be put away, and chickens fed and put up. I don't want to leave them out, and a day in the coop with clean water and fresh feed will be better for them. After that, I will scry for Jack's house, and I won't let the vision break on me. I will go to Jack's at dusk, when it is hopefully dark enough that I can sneak past him. It's a good plan. I tell myself it will work.

The chickens are looking at me balefully, knowing I'm not Amey. I scatter feed in their direction and carry the remainder of the water towards the creek, casting it across the muddied yard. I want to walk back up to the porch and sit, enjoy the sound of the wind in the trees and the water bubbling over rocks. Instead, I sit with the chickens, listening to them peck and scratch, letting my brain empty enough that the dread beating at me can recede for just a moment. Shadows creep across the yard, though there are hours of light yet, even down here in the holler. The chickens finish pecking at their foods and I herd them into their coop. I shut it up tight after moving their water inside. I don't know when I will be back for sure, and I don't want Gran to have to worry about it first thing in the morning.

It's as I shut the door, thinking of her, that I see the flowers.

They are growing at the back of the coop, where nothing was growing a moment before. They are purple, petals sprayed spots of brightness in the shade. I feel my heart clench, my stomach twist, my body go numb and distant.

Faintly, I smell lilacs.

I've started running before I've realized it. The wind casts clouds across the sun as I run up the hill, fighting gravity, knowing already it's too late. I have never planted irises in the yard. They mean too much to me—loss firstly. There's only one reason for them to be here, on the bank of this creek. I run, and the world narrows to me, to the hill, to my truck's dark green bleeding into the shadows beneath the trees. I pull my key ring out with fumbling fingers, slide into the cab. Jam the key into the ignition and turn.

The truck roars to life. I don't turn left, out towards the road.

I turn right. To Gran's house.

The trailer is still as I pull up, scattering gravel. The two rocking chairs on the porch sit empty. A gust of wind grabs the screen door, throwing it open. It closes with a harsh, desolate crack.

The creek is roaring in my head. I couldn't hear it before I opened the screen door, but I hear it now. There's no breath in my chest.

I find her in the kitchen.

She's wearing a lavender dress today, long white hair in a braid over her shoulder. On her back, she almost looks as if she's sleeping, but next to her is a picture frame, the glass cracked. I recognize the photo distantly—her, Archie, my mom, and Aunt Mae. She keeps it on the shelf next to the sink. There are dishes still sitting in the water, suds on her hands. No sign of violence. Just an old woman on the floor and the picture she grabbed for when she felt the world go out from under her.

I cross to her. Lilacs choke me. Archie is here, and there's an iris on Gran's chest. I know it's not really there. I know it's my sight. I brush it away anyway, frantic. Not irises, not now, not for her. The flower doesn't leave, of course. Whatever this is, whatever's gone wrong, I'm too late to change it. I know that. I put my hand where the flower should be. Feel her labored breathing under my palm.

"Hold on," I say, and I don't know if I'm talking to her or to me or to Archie. I don't know if I've said the words.

I need to get to the phone.

My body is moving as if it is underwater. Everything is slow, painful, cold. I step away from Gran, to the phone on the wall. There's time, I tell myself. There's time. She's breathing. The vision could be wrong. The phone is old, mounted on the wall, yellow as bone. I press the buttons, but I can't feel them under my fingers. I hear ringing.

"9-1-1. What's your emergency?"

"I need an ambulance," I say, give her my address and directions. Tell her that Gran is on the floor, unresponsive. The woman on the phone tells me to stay there, to stay on the line, and I tell her I can't keep the phone with me. It's got a chord. I can't keep it with me and be with Gran. I have to be with Gran.

When she protests, I hang up. I go back to where Gran is lying, and I take her hand.

CHAPTER FIVE

I CAN'T CALL GERRY.

That's what I think as I sit there, waiting for the ambulance, Gran's hand in mine. I can't call Gerry, because Gerry will know. Gerry will ask where Amey is, and I will have no answer, I will have nothing to give her, and she'll ask me questions. Gerry won't let me handle it myself—she doesn't much care for cops, but she's still from a place where you call the police to fix your problems. She doesn't know that Amey killed Randy, and she doesn't know I put his body in the woods for the trees and brambles to dig their roots into, and she will call the police, and then we will be over. I will go to jail, and Amey, too, if they believe me and can find her, and who will be there to take care of Gran?

Who can I call? I know I can't handle this on my own. It's a knowing that's distant. I've been near breaking before, have broken. I know I can't handle this because my insides feel like a ship that is tipping inexorably towards the water. The creek rushes and roars in the back of my head—it must be out of its banks now, the same way it was when Gran knew that she had to come pick me up from college three years ago, when everything fell apart. When the depression and the alcohol finally tipped me into the white roar of drowning, into the deeper water, the water I won't come back from. There are scars on my wrist from that night, and if Gran hadn't known, hadn't already been on her way, it would have been worse.

I remember when the smell of lilacs had come in ahead of her and brought my head up, when the door I'd left locked swung open and revealed her there, wind moving in her hair. The cinder block and tile hall, the fluorescents, the mundanity, had tried to make her something she wasn't, but she'd stood there with blue eyes like knives and like sky and like love. She stared me down until the blade dropped from my hand, and the shame that had been eating at me became grief and poured out of me the way it needed to. I'm still paying for that debt. I will never pay it.

She'd brought me back without questions or recrimination. And now here she lies, and I won't fail her again.

Gerry will ask questions. So I won't call Gerry.

I pat Gran's hand. Stand on leaden legs. It's like dreaming to walk to the phone, but I do it. The number I dial shouldn't be easy to remember, but it is. That's what happens when you find yourself falling for a man—you memorize his phone number even when you know better. He doesn't deserve to get involved with someone like me, and I aim to keep him out of things, I promised myself I would. But I dial his number anyway.

"Hello?" Owen says.

I have to swallow twice before I can answer.

"Owen, it's Rhia." My voice is normal, but my throat is trying to close up. I fight to breathe. I can't say it. "I need—"

My throat closes. I swallow again.

"Can you meet me at the hospital?"

"Rhia? Are you okay? Are you there now?" I can hear him moving already. I'm focusing on my breathing, because it is the only way I'm not sobbing into the phone, and I can't break down yet. Gran is here, and she needs me to hold it together. Distantly, I hear the sound of the sirens, coming for us both.

"It's Gran," I say, because I owe him that. Then, "The ambulance is here. I have to go."

"Okay," he says. "Rhia, I'll be there."

I hang up. I don't say goodbye.

Outside, the gravel crunches. Lights flash against the wall above my head. I turn just as the front door swings open. The paramedics go to my grandmother immediately, one bending to check her vitals, the other looking up at me. They're older than me, and I don't know them, and I am grateful for that.

"Rhiannon Blackburn?"

"Yes," I say.

"We need to get her stabilized," the other says, his voice grim. He's talking about Gran, and I remind myself to breathe, to breathe as they get her on the stretcher and lift her up. I follow them outside and watch as they put her in the box of the ambulance.

"Ma'am," says the first man, looking at me. He has the keys in his hand. The back doors of the vehicle are shut. "Are you driving, or riding with us?"

I blink my eyes, feeling the world move away from me.

"Ma'am?"

The creek roars and roars in my head. And something else, some bass sound more felt than heard. It is coming closer, that sound.

"I'll drive," I say.

The ambulance spins out on the gravel. I watch it go.

Water witches are supposed to be healers if you believe the stories, but if I've ever been healing inclined, I have never noticed. I make charms from wood, and I make simples and potions that can help folks with minor things—love and luck, strength sometimes. None of them are powerful, though. Amey can make curses, when she bothers to. She makes dolls and takes photos and lays workings on them, when someone gets under her skin, or at least she used to. I can't do that. I can see the future, a little, and the now if I look hard. I can listen. That's my strength.

Right now, I can't hear anything.

The truck rattles around me, eating up the road. I'm speeding, but I can't care enough to fix that. The ambulance is ahead of me, bright lights flashing red.

The hospital is white, white floors and white, white walls. I don't remember parking, and I don't remember the last part of the drive. Everything inside me is blank. I've never been in the hospital for any length of time, and the corridors wrap around me like tentacles pulling me in. One turn, then another, and all of it looks the same.

A nurse finds me. I think she's younger than me even, but my eyes can't focus on her face.

"My grandmother," I say, and she asks a name, and I say, "Clydie Ruth Blackburn." She walks me to a monitor, mumbles and shakes her head, tries to give me directions. There are pink flowers on her blue scrubs. I stare at them, her words floating by me.

I know, distantly, that I'm in shock, or something like it. I know this, but I can't pull free of the buzzing in my ears and behind my eyes.

"Rhiannon?"

The voice is familiar, but I don't recognize the face when I turn. Not immediately. This is a man in plain blue scrubs with a little pot belly.

"I thought that was you! What are you here for?"

I place him, then, and the familiarity helps break up the fog in my head. We went to high school together. His name is Rob, and he was in my honors math courses. Sometimes we traded notes. I remember those notes, and I remember long hours with books cracked open on the kitchen table, Gran puttering around in the kitchen while I worked. Sometimes, when she was done with her chores, she would stop to rub my back, like petting a cat.

"My Gran," I say. "The ambulance brought her."

His face changes, affability draining into sympathy, and I have to look at the ceiling because I need that fog, I need enough of it to keep going, and his expression will shatter it and leave me bare. When I look down again, his face is shuttered up like a house at night, and there's nothing in it that can hurt me.

"I'm going to take her down there," he tells the nurse behind me. She waves him on.

I follow Rob down through the twisting, white corridors. I see the signs, this time. They're on the walls, discreet. Nothing my misted eyes could catch.

~

Sometime later, I'm seated in the waiting room. There are no windows. A television is murmuring in the corner, and hospital staff pass by from time to time. The sounds are distant.

I feel like the ground is giving out under me, like I'm on an elevator going down, sinking forever into the cold earth just like Randy did. I hang my head, waiting. Waiting for the doctors to come back, waiting for them to tell me what I already know. I was too late. Gran is gone. Everything is cold and distant, and I am lost. I'm so lost. How can I ever be strong enough for this?

I realize, at some point, that I'm staring at someone's boots. I lift my head.

It's Owen, and for a minute, I can't understand how he is here in front of me. The overwhelming light of the hospital hall washes out his tan, so he looks yellow and pale. I stare at him, and I can't find words anywhere in my chest. There's nothing there. Nothing to come out.

"Let's get you something to eat," he says.

This is a truism in all parts of the South, that when things are terrible, people's first thought is to feed you. Owen has brought hamburgers. They are nothing special—fast food wrapped in cheap paper—but the smell hits me, and I find that I'm ravenous. The hunger isn't welcome. I don't want it. But I can't reject his offer, so when he sits down and puts the first burger in my hand, I eat it, wooden. If half of what I'm eating is tears and snot, well, I'm pretty sure Owen isn't going to go tattle on me about it. Still, I don't like acting like this in front of him, and that makes me tear up more, until I can't see, can't breathe for crying.

"Hey, hey," he says, taking the half-eaten burger out of my hands. My whole body is shuddering like a tree in a storm, and that makes me think of Gran, and I cry harder as he wraps his arms around me. He's wearing flannel, and it's soaked through by the time I settle back to weeping instead of outright sobs. He doesn't say anything like "it'll be alright" or "don't cry," and I'm grateful for that because I can't even look at him, can't speak, can't do anything. I feel like I'm going to shatter. I feel like I'm paper in a flood.

He hands me back the burger when the tears are done. I finish it, even though it's gone cold and mushy, and I drink the water he's brought, too.

When the doctor comes, I don't cry. I sit stoically and listen to him and Owen talk, catching words like "stroke" and "too long" and "not responsive" and "palliative." Normal words for ending a life. And I'm grateful that the crying has already happened, grateful that Owen is here to ask questions in my place.

Owen goes with me to see Gran, which is good. I don't think I would get through it otherwise.

She's on a bed, and she looks small, lying under a thin yellow blanket. They've taken off the lilac dress and put her in a hospital gown that's a pale, washed-out blue. She looks so frail in the bed, her long white braid down her wrinkled, bare shoulder, like a woman made out of cobwebs and sticks. The machines keeping her breathing beep and bleat. I know, looking at her, that if she's still in there, she isn't really there at all, but I take her hand anyway. It's cold, and I chafe the soft skin as if I could give her any warmth of mine. As if the magic worked like that. With her eyes closed, her life gone, I see how old she is, her whole body like crinkled silk, like a parachute that has no wind to open it. I am numb, and the breath is coming hard in my chest, like my lungs have forgotten how to breathe. I have to think about it, pull in and out. In and out, with the beeping of the machine.

"Of all the times, Gran," I say, and then regret saying it even though it's true. Of all the times for her to go and try dying. Amelie will never forgive herself if she's not here.

And she's not going to be here. Matter of fact, she may follow Gran into death, if I can't save her. My heart pounds and stutters in my chest.

"Rhia," Owen says, "Rhia, breathe."

He sounds so much like her.

I let go of Gran's hand, let him sit me down. I don't want to be weak. I don't want to be crying in front of him, and I don't want Gran to be dead. Breaking down again fills me with frustration. It's like coming home to a freshly mopped floor that's been trampled all over with mud, or finishing a beautiful carving project and dropping it down the stairs so it's all scuffed up and broken. I've just put myself back together, I've listened to that damned doctor tell me she's not going to wake up and not cracked, and this, this is the thing I can't handle, her in the bed, her small, her breathing but gone.

I let out a sound that's animal, muffled in my palm. Nausea is a fist in my gut. I've doubled over, and I'm biting my thumb like it will help to feel the pain. Owen is trying to comfort me, and isn't that something, him seeing me like this. But it's not his calm voice or his hand on my back that lets me breathe again.

It's the smell of lilacs.

"I need a minute," I tell him. My voice is tight in my throat, fogged by tears and grief.

"Are you sure you want to be alone?" he asks. It's not him trying to protest, that much is clear. I look up at him, meet his eyes even though it's powerfully hard to do it and not dissolve again. The smell of lilacs is still in the air, though, and I know I need him gone, for all I want to cling to him.

"I'll be fine," I tell him. "I just need a minute. To talk to her."

His expression clears in understanding.

"I'll go find you something to drink," he says. His eyes are still worried, but he gives me a reassuring half-smile. Then he casts another glance at my grandmother's body and leaves, pulling the privacy curtain behind him but not the door. I can hear the noises of nurses and aids in the hall, can hear the call bell from some other room. Can hear the beeping of the machines keeping Gran's body alive.

But she's not in there anymore, not really.

"I'm ready," I say.

The ghost that appears in front of me is Archie's. I don't realize how much I've been hoping until I see him, but his pleasant face almost makes me cry again. It's hard to think of Archie as Grandpa, even though that's what he is. His ghost is so young, not much older than me, though he was a lot older than that when he died. His face is concerned, like Owen's was. They've got something similar in the eyes, I think.

He sits on the edge of Gran's bed. I don't expect to feel anything when he takes my hands, and I suck in a breath thick with flower-smell instead of hospital fumes. His grip is cold and paper-dry. I don't realize I'm trembling until he shushes me.

"Rhiannon," he says, smiling gently. "Your Gran sent me to talk to you."

"Why?" I say. "Why not come herself?" It's a child's desperate plea. Archie's expression doesn't change, but he shakes his head gently.

"Showing yourself to the living is hard stuff, especially if you ain't really dead. Ruth isn't dead yet, Rhiannon."

"She's not coming back," I tell Archie, saying the words to kill the hope already blossoming in my chest.

"No," he says, "she's not."

I swallow. Remember Gran telling me to breathe just yesterday. It's like her voice is in my ear, and maybe it is. I do what she says.

Archie waits.

"I was a water witch, too, you know," he says, when he thinks I'm ready. "You'd think a wind witch and a water witch would make more water or wind, but your momma was fire from the day she was born. When she had you, I thanked all the stars you weren't hers. She was glad, too, but not for the reasons you think. Fire witch is hard business. She didn't want that for you. But she wanted you to be loved, to be among family, so she gave you to me and your Gran. She thought I could help you. I hoped I could. But then I went and died before you were old enough to hardly remember me and left your Gran to do all the work." His smile is rueful, his grip tight. I can feel my fingers going colder and colder, but I don't pull away.

"Rhiannon, you're one of the most powerful water witches I've ever seen. I've watched you grow up, girl, and convince yourself that you aren't special. You are. Your Gran knew it. I know it. And you know what you have to do now."

I've been looking at our hands, but I look up now. My eyes are wide. I know what he is talking about, one witch to another. I know. In the part of myself where my magic lives, I hear the high notes of the creek, distant and soft. Beneath that? Beneath that, there's deeper waters.

"Archie, I can't. I can't."

"You can, my pony girl. And what's more, you must, if you want to save Amey." He's still smiling, but he's earnest, and the nickname I'd half forgotten brings warmth to fight the cold fear in my chest. "You're afraid. Let me tell you a secret?"

I nod, feeling my lips tremble.

"All the living are afraid, Rhiannon, and many of the dead. There's no shame in fear. Only in what you let it make of you." He stands, still gripping my hands. His lips are like snowflakes on my forehead, cold, cold.

Then he's gone.

Owen comes back a few minutes later to find me chafing my hands, staring at Gran. He hands me a coffee. I accept it, glad for the warmth.

"I didn't know if you took creamer," he says.

"A little," I tell him, wedging the coffee between my thighs and taking the packet he offers me. There's a little wooden stirring stick, too. I stir the creamer in, then raise it to cradle in my hands once more. My eyes are still on Gran's face, memorizing it.

I take a drink of the coffee, feeling it scald my tongue. Think of my mother, out there somewhere in the world, maybe, or dead maybe, too. I hadn't thought of her in years before yesterday, but I wonder now if she knows that Gran is dying. If she could heal her where I can't, lay on the hands and call the sickness from her and burn it up.

"Thank you," I say to Owen, trying to break the chain of my thoughts. He's still standing, and I stand, too, leaving my coffee, stepping towards Gran. "Thank you for coming here. I couldn't think of who else to call."

"Did you tell Gerry yet?" he asks. I'm surprised, but I shouldn't be. He knows Gerry and I are close. It's just not something a man would usually think to ask.

"I will. They can keep her going a long time like this." I reach down to take Gran's hand, my own no longer numb from cold. "As long as we need."

Owen has nothing to say to that, and I don't blame him. I study Gran's face a few minutes more before I turn to him.

Archie was right. I know what I have to do.

"Owen," I say. "I have to go get Amey, and I may be a while. I know it's a lot to ask, but—"

"I'll stay here," he says.

I look at him, brown eyes, curls, laugh lines, the strong nose and jaw. I think that if we make it through this, Amey and I, that I'll be needing to tell her about him. And to tell him about us. About what it means, to be a witch. I'm not willing to leave him alone anymore, and I don't know when that changed.

"Thank you," I say, half whispered. Then I step towards him and let him fold me in his arms, just for a moment. Savor the warmth of him wrapping around me, and hope I'll get to feel its like again.

He kisses my hair, and lets me go.

I leave without looking back.

CHAPTER SIX

THE FIRST TIME I heard the river sing, I was seven and trying to catch minnows. The sun was coming down sharp and just a little too warm on my back, my hands were in the water up to my elbows, and I was lying on my belly, silent and still, waiting. The boat beneath me rocked slightly from the water, and the light moving on the river had nearly lulled me to sleep. I was keeping awake with my goal, though. I wanted to catch a fish with my bare hands.

The boat belonged to the family of one of my few childhood friends, a second or third cousin from Gran's side of the family who hadn't figured out how weird I was yet, maybe because I wasn't. Before seven, I very rarely heard or saw things that no one else could, just the things most any child can. Children hear better than adults, I think, so if you're good at hearing things that are quiet, like trees and rivers and rocks, you don't stick out quite as much. Me and my friend Teddy would play with dolls and action figures—he had a bunch of dinosaurs that made noises when you pushed the buttons on them, of which I was envious—and run around the backyard slinging mud at one another and climbing trees. Amey would come live with me the next week, and Gran would stop bringing me over to Teddy's house as much since he and Amey didn't get along so well. A couple of years later, Teddy would die of appendicitis, leaving the earth too soon as bright-burning souls often do. I loved that kid like I loved the stars in the sky. His was the first funeral I went to, and I will never forget the pastor in black, the wails, the raised hands, the too-small casket all polished and the bouquet of purple irises I held clenched in my small fists until it was time to lay them on the casket. Gran had gripped my hand when I did as if I might float away and leave her there.

But that would be years later. My hands were in the water, now, and Teddy was sleeping safe in his bed in his parents' doublewide. There were bees in the flowers, and the water rippled with light as the breeze came up and stole some of the heat from my skin.

In that moment, the sound of the river on the rocks changed.

It's something that happens all the time, if you're listening. The sound changes—slight enough that you may not realize you've heard it the first few times it happens. The scientific explanation is that the water volume has varied—a dam has let out upriver, maybe, or a storm's leavings finally made it down to you. And that's not wrong. The river changes her song for all sorts of reasons, or his song. Rivers don't really have gender. It doesn't matter, but the river is so big, so vast, that I want to make it seem smaller. I want it to be a person I can talk to, not a spirit as old as the hills.

The sound of the river changed, and I lifted my head. Looked across the water to the far forested bank and the mountains beyond. And the river spoke.

I can't tell you what it's like for a river to speak, except to say it's like your bones are giving a rattling hum. It's the feeling you get when you're holding tight to someone you love, praying to never let go. It's like someone just tried on your skin, or maybe like someone just changed you into something that no longer fits in skin at all, and you're rising and falling and splitting apart and coming together all at once.

I can't tell you what it's like when the river speaks. I can tell you that after that day, I didn't put my toes in the water, or my hands, or my hair, even though all I wanted in the whole world was to do just that. When Amey came, I was glad for someone to ground me in home. The only time I regretted it was when Teddy died, but I still didn't try to go back. The fear was too big.

My truck is trundling down the road now, and the river is coming closer. I'm listening for it, and it is listening back to me. I can feel it feel my grief. And my rage. I can hear the sound of the water change.

At last, I know that I will change with it.

There's pull-offs along this road, gravel and dirt packed down by plenty of cars before. The road is narrow, unlined, almost in the water, a thin thread connecting two hollers, but occasionally the land juts out. When that land is high enough to be dry and the guardrail is missing, people drive out on it. Everyone loves the river—fishermen, kayakers, babies, it doesn't matter. You can be poor, rich, young, old—the river has a place for you. In the summer, I might not find parking. But summer is dying and the day is nearly done. There's no one else down here.

I pull my truck into one of the pull-offs, step out. The air is cool down here next to the water, fall air, and some of the leaves are already turning. The sound of the river is loud in my ears, echoing from the rapids downstream, but it is quiet here. The sandy earth is scattered with bits of glass and cinders from a fire pit someone has put together. I'm glad, distantly, that I'm still in my boots. You never know what you might find in the earth around here.

The truck door is still open, and I left my keys in it. I should close it, but I'm already walking, and the rocks are under my boots, jutting out over the water like a plank I'm stepping on to. I don't look back.

It's deep here. The water is gray and black and transparent, showing glimmers of sandy riverbed far below. The green and muck that might have filled it at other times is dying out this late in the year. It yields a flat surface, a mirror for the bright blue of the sky, and for my face.

"Help me," I say to the river. "Help me save her. I can't lose Amey, too." I have nothing to bargain with. Nothing to give but myself. But that is the only thing the river would ever take.

I let myself fall.

That fall should be quick. Instead, it is slow, slow as molasses on a spoon. I tip forward, I feel the press of gravity catch me. I can see my face in the flat water. There's no expression on it—no fear, no anything. It's like me and my body and the river are balanced together in this moment, even though I know the decision is already made. There's no going back. Only through.

The water hits me.

It's a slap just as my eyes close, and it takes me by surprise. I inhale, a quick, watery gasp. Cold presses into my hair, into my pores, into my nose and mouth and lungs.

I open my eyes.

When you open your eyes underwater, the world is blurry, vague. This is not that. This is clear—and I am not seeing what I meant to see.

There is no riverbed, no soft mud, no rocks. No fish swim about my head. This is blackness, and it is clear, and through it is coming—something. There are no words for what is coming, and I feel my throat close and my whole self fight to clench against it. Press that fight down, bare my throat, and let it come.

The river climbs inside me then, silver as glass, puts on my skin and shows me forever.

~

I see myself.

I see myself on the night that everything was darkness.

Perhaps it makes sense that that is the first place I go when the river takes me down the smooth flow of has-beens and could-bes. Perhaps it makes sense that, in the darkest part of a dark day, when desperation drives me at last into the arms of a thing that has waited for me forever, I am closest to another darkness. The darkness of alone is not so different from the darkness of loss. With loss, you are missing those you love. Alone, you are missing yourself.

I've never been a good companion to myself. Perhaps that is why, when I was twenty and trying on adulthood for the first time, I failed so spectacularly. At home, with Gran and Amey to keep me myself, I had known the boundaries of who I was. When I left, at last, with two years of community school classes under my belt and a certainty that I was going to make something of myself—well, you can't really make something of yourself, can you? You are something, no matter what you do.

"I wondered when you would make it back here."

It's my own voice, but it's younger. She—I—am sitting on the bed of my small dormitory room. The sheets haven't been washed in weeks. There is grease in my long, black hair. My face is gaunt as a bone. The smell of the place, the smell of stress and despair and alcohol sweat, is an odor I could have gone without smelling again for the rest of my life. I look into my own blue-gray eyes and know that this girl has been living down inside my heart for three years.

I don't want anything to do with her.

I turn around, spinning to look at the off-white walls. The river is humming in the back of my head, and I can't decide if that is a comfort or if it makes me want to spit nails. It brought me here.

"You brought you here," the girl says. I whirl. "What, you don't think I know everything you're thinking? You're not really here, and I'm not really here. This is all about you. You brought you here, and you made me, and here we are."

There's a knife in her hand. I know it, and the knowing makes me cold. I've been sitting with that knife ever since I knew my mother was never coming back for me, ever since I knew I was worth leaving. I know what happens with it, if Gran doesn't come to stop me. I look back towards the door. It doesn't open.

"So you save me, Rhia," she says. The knife spins between her fingers, a trick Teddy taught me when we were kids together. I only ever did it playfully. There's nothing playful in this other me's face.

"I've got Amey to save," I grind out. "I don't have time for this. You should know that."

"I'm not the one who decides what you have time for," the girl says. The knife spins again. "Besides, when did Amey come to save us? Where was Amey when I needed her? All she ever does is mess things up. Make everyone hate you in that bullshit town. Get herself kidnapped, kill a man."

The words give me chills. I remember it. I remember that night, sitting in this room. My gaze goes to the papers on the floor, marked in red. To the bottle of Jack Daniels that was mostly drained. I'd thought of pills and decided against it. Decided I wanted to do things brave.

"That's not true. Amey was living her life," I say. "She was doing her best. She always does her best."

"Amey was fucking her boyfriend," says the younger me, but she doesn't sound angry. She sounds sad. "And it wouldn't have mattered. She couldn't save me. She couldn't save Gran."

I swallow at that. I feel grief, but anger, too, and for the first time, I realize it's not just for me. Amey did this, too. Amey has gone and gotten herself caught up in things, and so she can't be here to help me. If she were here, none of this would have happened. This is too big for me, losing Gran is too big, and I'm so small.

But I forgive her. I always have forgiven her, for everything. Because I love Amey.

I can love myself, too.

I remember being on the bed, the alcohol buzzing in my veins, blurring the edges, knife in my hand. I remember deciding that it was better if I died, because I had taken all our savings and all our hopes and dashed them running after something like acceptance. It had been so hard to make friends, just like it always was, only I hadn't realized how much it would hurt to have to find that out all over again. That I wasn't wanted. That I was different. I'd thrown myself at acceptance like it would save me, and before I knew it, I had failed my classes and pissed away my scholarships, and I was still, always, alone.

I take a deep breath then. Cross to the bed. Sit down with the girl with long, unwashed hair and desperate, lonely eyes.

"I'll take that," I say. She grips the knife, tight, brandishes it between us. I smile. Fold my hand around hers. She is trembling.

"We are stronger than you think," I tell her. "We don't need a knife, not anymore." She jerks, like she's trying to cut me, but I've got a good grip. I've been eating, and I've spent three years working with my hands. I keep her hand in mine, point the knife away from us both, and wrap her up in my arms.

"Failure is a piece of living," I say.

"I don't want to lose," says the girl, and I feel that grief like it's my own, because it is. I've always been trying to grip tight to things that can't be held onto.

I think of Gran, of the moment when she walked into this room. I've never asked her how she knew to come get me, and now I'll never get to. It doesn't matter. She knew, and she came. I say her words, and at last I know that they are true.

"You can never be alone, girl. I'm always with you."

The river roars then, and I hear its words with my bones more than with my head.

And now, I, too.

~

I'm in a whirlpool, and the whirlpool is light. It's sun on the water, and there's someone here with me.

"Why me?" I ask the water. It rushes and tumbles, light as a feather but holding the weight of ages. Water is renewed each day, each hour. Rises, becomes rain, falls. The river casts off atoms the way a child does, and calls them back to itself.

Potential, says the river, or something like it. But that's not quite right—it's like rain on the water, maybe, speckling everything with newness. I'm just a drop, or maybe I'm a thunderstorm. The river's been around a while; it's not great with metaphors.

"Alright then," I say. "You don't care I might kill a man tonight?"

I feel cold, deep currents, the kind light never touches. I feel laughter.

Of course, I should have known the river takes the same as it gives. I wonder if it will take me.

Someday, says the river, and I know someday is maybe today or maybe when I'm eighty, and that I'll get little say in the matter. My bones will go to the rocks, my tendons to the fish. That's the cost of doing business.

And I know, too, that I don't much care. I think of Amey's red hair and laughing eyes, and of how much I love her, no matter that she's not always perfect. That's what siblings do. What I was always going to do for her. They pay the cost.

"Take me back," I tell the river.

The river does.

CHAPTER SEVEN

MOUNTAINS HAVE DEEP, dark hearts, and those hearts are carved by water.

The river is thrumming in my blood when I come to myself, dripping, on the bank. I'm standing. I do not remember standing; I do not remember climbing free of the wet. I am simply here, born on the sandy shore. My breath hisses in and out of my wet lips. The air is cold.

Across the river, mountains slope down to meet the water in smooth curves. They are green still, despite the chill that has made the air brisk. I see the dark reflection of them, broken up by silvering rapids.

I feel, beneath that reflection, the water rushing over rocks. It is like feeling my heart pound in my chest. The water moves through me, a roar, a tumbling.

"Enough to drive a body mad," I say, and suddenly I'm back in myself, wet and cold on the riverbank.

Being back in my skin should feel safe. It doesn't. My body crawls with the need to be moving. There are flickers in the corner of my vision—red leaves, purple flowers, the signs of struggle. I need to move. There's not much time. Already the sun is nearly gone. Golden light is fading into silver, the sky beginning to blush above me. It's time.

Rhia. Hurry.

Whatever Jack intends, he will do it tonight. I can feel it now, the pressure of the future—the path time moves in like a river in its banks.

I cup my hand, pull against the river like an anchor on the line. The water dripping from my hair and clothes accretes to itself, returns to the riverbank. A small puddle of it pools in my palm. I pull a vial from my pocket, let the river water trickle inside. Just in case.

Dry now, I move for the truck. Gravel spits as I peel out of the pull-off, and I turn my nose for the mountain.

~

Driving up this road is like driving in a dream. It is like, and not like, the blankness that took me on the way to the hospital. There's a sense of inevitability to this climb. The future flickers and flashes, like sunlight slanting through bare branches, drawing me forward into the dusk.

If you had asked me a few hours ago where Jack lived, I could have told you an approximation. I've never been to visit him, though. I would not have been able to describe the lay of the land his house sits on, or the small, concrete-floored building behind that house like a dead blot on the earth. I could not have told you there is a pull-off, a dead-end road used for ATVs and hunters, just down the road from his house, one that's perfect to hide a large, green truck that needs a wash. But I know all that now, and I pull in under the trees, some just starting to edge to yellow and orange. The cold's finally gotten to them, just like me.

Gravel pops under my boots, and I shut the truck's cab quietly, listening. There's just forest sounds, and the river whispering in my blood. I can tell that it doesn't know for sure what's coming, and I can also tell that it doesn't mind that. There's no fear in the river. Just a waterfall of certain fate, for me, for Jack, for Amey and Marie. Water flows downhill, draws down, grounds down. There's only one ending for all of us.

But water also buoys, for a while.

I climb through the trees, feeling the little springs and streams deep under my feet. The slope is steep. My boots slide on leaf and loam as I scramble myself up the rise to where Jack's house sits on a wide, cleared lot of grass going tall with neglect.

It's not dark yet, but there's a thin sort of quality to the light that means there's not much of it left. The sky is a bruised blue-gray fading to indigo. Lights shine from inside the house, and I step back into the deepening shadows of the forest, trusting them to hide me while I get a feel for the place. There, the house, a squat, small thing with peeling paint and creeper running up the walls. There, the garage, detached, large, and closed up tight. There's probably a padlock. The windows have certainly been boarded up. It sits on a concrete pad, and I can guess that's where he's keeping her. She's close, I know that. I feel the shape of her like a stone in the path of the water, shunting the current aside. One soul that will always belong to the earth.

There's cover in this field where Jack's house sits, and that's good news. I cast my eyes about. An old, beat-up Chevy is sitting not far from me, grass grown up around it, and a few old tires. There's a big pile of brush between me and the driveway, which snakes up from the bottom of the valley, where the road runs alongside a small stream I can hear burbling, foreign yet familiar, in my blood. Looks like Jack is planning a bonfire at some point, and it's a good time of year for it, with the nights cool but not too dry. Either of these objects might be enough to shield me from sight during my approach to the shed.

There's no sign of a dog, which puts one of my fears to rest. I pull a vial from my pocket, uncork it with a held breath. The creek is still somewhere back in the back of my head, wrapped all up in the river sounds, but it's faint. I'm not sure I could have heard it before I went down to the river. I keep myself still and quiet, search for the sound of it, let it flow.

The mist boils up out of the vial like a ghost. I inhale, smooth and even. Exhale, and it travels out over the grass between me and Jack's house. Do I imagine that the breeze, such as there was, goes still? Is there a faint scent of lilac around me?

I don't have time to ponder it. There's gravel crunching, and a truck drives up, headlights nearly cutting through the darkness that shelters me. It's newer, a dark color—probably black, but it's hard to say in the light. I start back, barely keeping myself from running back into the trees and giving myself away. Motion attracts the eye; anyone who lives out in the country for a while learns that quick. Stillness is my friend, here. So I stay still, even though it feels like I am far too visible. The mist is still low to the ground, and I will it to grow, to spread and draw the moisture in the cool earth into itself. Surprisingly, it does what I ask.

I spot azaleas under the trees, an orange glare of caution out of season. I take two slow, smooth steps further into the trees, trusting the mist to obscure me. Then the front door opens. Jack steps out.

He's an unassuming man, Jack. Maybe that is what makes him so frightening. He's not very tall, and he's wiry, not big. Not ugly, either. Nothing makes him particularly memorable until you've seen him move. Jack is fast, faster than a snake striking, and he's got a tongue sharper than a skinning knife. His eyes, when you meet them, are flat unless he's trying to charm you, and they sparkle when he's hurting a body. I know this because I've seen him beat a man nearly half to death at Spike's, and because I've been on the receiving end of his insults from time to time. Mostly, though, I stay clear of Jack and Jack has no interest in me.

Would that Amey had known better, but Amey wouldn't know better if it hit her upside the head. And I can't blame her, entirely, for falling in love. Hearts can run away with you sometimes. Even here, in this misty field with a night of uncertainty in front of me and loss fresh on my tongue, my heart leaps at the thought of Owen's eyes. I note it, and I let it go.

If I live, and Amey lives, I hope he'll kiss my hair again.

Jack has come down from the porch. He's got jeans on and a faded T-shirt, and what are no doubt cowboy boots, even to tromp around out here. Two men get out of the truck to greet him. They seem familiar but I can't place them in the dimness. Not the kind of folks who come out to the farmer's market, apparently, nor young enough for me to have gone to school with. Probably some of Jack's friends from the bar or work. I don't know what they're here for. Seems like a bad idea to have a party when your wife and her girlfriend are chained up in the shed, but Jack's got an ego. Maybe he doesn't think anyone will notice. Or maybe they know exactly what Jack's been up to these past two days and are coming to see the show. The thought makes my stomach clench.

There's more crunching on the drive. The mist is thickening, so the sound bounces, but I see the headlights of another car. It parks. A door slams. The smell of whiskey drifts to me. The men mill around, drinking deep, voices holding an element of menace I don't understand.

Not until Jack lifts a Tiki torch out of the big black truck. He gestures. One of the newcomers takes it, and he reaches for another. I look to the stack of brush and old wood perched in the middle of his yard. The dark has thickened now—things are blurry at the edges with lack of light. The mist has crawled across nearly to Jack's house. I hear one of the men remark on it. Someone pulls out a lighter, touches it to one of the torches. I see another man chug something in a metal can, crunch it up, and toss it in the yard. Jack slings his arm around that one's neck, offers him something I can't make out through the mist and growing dark, except the smell of skunk and something sweet comes to me, and I know it's drugs to go with all that liquor.

These men mean to do something that requires liquid courage. They're prepared and excited, probably have guns, and if any of them are sober, I'll lick my boot. I stare at the giant pile of brush, brain gone blank.

What do you do to punish a witch? I've always known the answer. But I've been operating under the assumption that Jack was worried about being caught, that he was afraid. This isn't fear, not on his part. It's meanness. How does he plan to keep this quiet? But maybe these men don't fully know what they're in for. Maybe they think Jack will stop at hurting Amey, at scaring her. And people are always less likely to believe a living woman than a dead one.

Someone turns on some music. It's a song I like, but I imagine after tonight I'll never want to hear it again. Johnny Cash, singing about fire. It breaks me from my shock, and I pull on the mist, pull it up, the river roaring in my chest.

I only know of one sure way to deal with fire. You drown it.

The river is unafraid, so my fear seems small. Shadows grow and stretch across the hollow. There's still light in the sky, but none of it quite reaches the ground. I exhale. Then I creep out into the darkness, movements slow and liquid, like an eddy in the mist that wraps itself around me. The men are laughing, drinking, voices too-loud with anticipation and alcohol. If I can just get to Amey, just get her feet on the ground, all of this will be over. We'll vanish into the night.

"Let's get this party started, boys," I hear Jack say. I'm two steps from the old truck, and I duck behind it, hitting the dirt. There's no shout. No one's seen me. I roll underneath and army-scramble up to the edge closest to the garage so I can see.

There are at least three who've come to help Jack with what he aims to do. Two vehicles, but I didn't see who exited the second one. The mist is thick, and I can't see through it any better than they can, so I can't see their faces. Still, their voices surround me in the fog. The river is murmuring hints and tricks at me, trying to tell me what is coming, but my heart is so far up my throat I think it's behind my eyeballs. I can't hear anything with it pounding in my ears, except the crackle-swish of grass and the heavy footsteps going by my head as someone makes their way to the garage. To Amey, alone in the dark. I hear the padlock fall to the dirt.

She comes out screaming.

I know Amey, and this scream is not scared. This scream is rage. She punches Jack in the nose. His head whips back, and I almost think she's going to make it past him. I'm tensed, ready to haul myself up, ready to run out from under there and do what I don't know. The river wells in my head, and my muscles lock before I can dart forward.

Jack punches her back. Her scream chokes off in her throat.

Jack grabs her and slings her over his shoulder. She's too dazed to call her magic to her. Marie comes running behind. Another man catches her by the elbows as she screams at Jack. There's only Jack and the man holding Marie over here, I realize over the roaring in my ears. The rest are next to the fire, getting it started. And Jack is distracted. Amey's already started shouting curses again, voice ragged.

Now, the river says.

I roll out from under the truck and boil up from the ground. Jack's already turning, Amey pounding futilely at his back. He's pulling a gun from his belt, and behind him, Marie is lunging against the other man's grip. She's screaming and crying and Amey is cursing and the gun comes free, and I don't know what he's planning to do, but I know he can't be allowed to do it. There's no time to think.

I hit him with every ounce of momentum I can muster in ten feet.

I'm not a small girl, not anymore. But the man is made of iron, and he barely staggers. Still, his hand flies to the side. The gun goes off, and the bullet catches the man holding Marie high in the shoulder. He screams.

Jack moves fast as lightning, bringing the gun back down towards my head. I see it coming but I can't dodge. His fist takes up my whole vision.

Impact. I see black and white and red.

The ground hits me. I roll. It's instinct, and it doesn't come from me but from the water that knows motion best. I hear thunks in the earth beside my head, half an instant before the report of the gun echoes like thunder off the trees. I scramble to my feet.

Jack's got the gun on me.

For a moment, all I can see is the barrel of it. Even in the dimness, the flickering, distant firelight rapidly becoming the strongest illumination, the barrel of that gun seems to shine. I feel my vision narrow to a pinprick.

Amey rears up like a cobra and wraps an arm around Jack's eyes. The gun goes off. I feel something punch me in the leg, feel myself spin with the force of it. The pain comes after.

The men by the fire are shouting and moving in our direction. I sure as shit hope Jack is done shooting at things until he can reload because I didn't come armed for a shootout. I am not a shootout kind of girl. There is blood pooling in the fabric of my jeans, heavy wet rapidly going cold. I put a palm on it and I tell that blood to stay where it is. My head spins. I think I'm in shock.

Jack throws Amey down, kicks her hard. She lies still. My shock vanishes into fury.

I pick myself up out of the grass and draw a vial from my pocket.

"Jack Higgins," I say, and my voice is the roar of water.

Everything goes quiet. Jack and I look at one another in the gathering dark. Marie is crying, panicky, gasping breaths somewhere to my right, and there is a groaning from the man Jack shot. The other two men have frozen in place. One turns, running for the driveway.

The stopper of the vial of river water pops free under my thumb.

"Should have known your sister was a witch, too," Jack says to me, and he kicks Amey again to punctuate his point. She groans. "You think you can magic her free? I'll shoot you first, and no one will even look for you. Everyone hates you, Rhia."

He is coming towards me as he talks, the gun held casually in his hand. Not pointed at me, not yet. He doesn't think I'm a threat now, with the blood running down my leg. I let him come. I don't think that my leg will take my weight, and I need concentration. I need everything I have.

Water pools in my palm.

"Should have stayed away, Rhia," he says, reaching for me, his teeth cutting the dark with a grin. The gun comes up at last.

I slap the water to his face and I tell it where to go.

The river water feels like an appendage as it burrows into his lungs.

He hits me, of course. This is the second hit I've taken to the head with the butt of that gun, though it's glancing compared to the last.

My body folds, dropping me on my belly in the dirt, but I hold on to the voice of the river, hold on to what I want, my fingers fisting in the grass. The only way out of this is through. If Jack gets up, I don't. I hear his lungs sucking fruitlessly at the air, hear the last man shout, hear boots coming running. Jack convulses, heels drumming against the ground, but gasp as he might, no air can reach his lungs. The water has laid claim. He belongs to us, to the river and I. The outcome is inevitable.

I smell the moment he dies, when his body lets go of all the things it's been holding onto. There's a moment of silence, when the only panting breath is my own. In that stillness, I hear the river sigh in contentment. I don't have the energy to be afraid of its delight.

The ground beneath me trembles and bucks—Amey—and suddenly the two remaining men start screaming like babies. I pull my head up with effort. Peer through the mist and the fire-flicked black, but my vision blurs and I can't see anything anyway. I hear car doors slam, and the spitting of gravel as the pair of vehicles peel off down the mountain.

The weight of Jack's life is settling in my gut like a stone, and I lower my head back into the dirt. I killed him. They know it. I should stop them the same way, but I won't.

And anyway, my leg and my head hurt like the dickens.

"Rhia," Amey shouts, and then she's rolling me over. I groan, feeling my head throb at the motion.

"I'm fine," I tell her. "Go check on Marie."

"You're not fine, you're not fine." She's crying, I think. I can feel the tears on her face, saltwater, in the same part of me that I can feel the river. It's a strange enough experience to make me drift, for a minute, before I push the cotton out of my brain enough to answer.

"Amey, you okay?"

She gives something like a laugh and something like a sob.

"Yeah, I'm fucking okay," she says. "You killed that bastard good."

The music must have been coming from one of the vehicles that just left because it's quiet up here now. There's frogs singing somewhere, and night bugs. I remind my blood it's supposed to stay in my body, remind my body that it's stronger than it thinks it is.

"Help me get up," I say to Amey, and we stagger upwards together, her under my arm on my bad side. She's limping too, I think, and it makes our walking jumbled. We get to Marie together, who's just sitting in the grass staring. I can't blame her. I stand as Amey kneels and wraps her in her arms.

"Baby, baby, it's okay, we're okay," she says.

"Is he—" Marie starts. Then, "Did you?" I can tell in her voice she doesn't know what to want. Can tell there's blame for whoever killed her husband waiting to bloom right alongside the gratitude.

"It wasn't Amey that did it," I say.

Marie looks up at me, I think. It's getting really dark now, so it's hard to tell exactly with her shadowed by Amey and I and the garage. But life comes back into her. She takes a deep breath, even though it hitches in her throat, and she stands.

"I want to see," she says.

We're a sorry lot, limping over to stand over Jack's slack body. It's the only body—all those other boys have left. I'd be more worried about that, but there's only so much worry a body can handle.

Jack is a dim shape in the grass, looking smaller in death. Marie stares down at him, and I cling to Amey, not sure I'm going to be able to keep standing much longer. I lost a lot of blood before I told it to stay put, and I hurt everywhere there is to hurt. Amey pokes him with her toe, and I can tell she wants to do more, but she doesn't want to hurt Marie's feelings. Marie just stares.

The bonfire settles, throwing up sparks and spits of fire. For a moment, his staring eyes are shown in sharp relief. I think that I will remember this moment for the rest of my life, even after all the other wounds have healed.

"Alright," Marie says at last.

Together, we start our long journey down the mountain.

CHAPTER EIGHT

It's a long walk back to my truck.

Marie walks with us. She can't bring herself to go back into the house, and I don't know if I blame her. There must not have been a lot of love for her here, and likely there was a whole lot of fear instead. I don't argue about it, but I do wish she had gotten the keys to her car at least. Each jouncing step Amey and I take moves like fire through my leg and head. I swear I can feel my pulse in my eye sockets. I've put the poultice I made for endurance and strength on all three of our lips. I can guess they haven't eaten since Jack threw them in there, though he must have given them water somehow. Both of them look gaunt, and the walk to the bottom of the driveway leaves them nearly as spent as me, even with the earth-bitter herbs to add strength to our steps.

We don't speak as we walk. I start to, a few times, but the things I have to tell Amey cling to the insides of my throat. I'm too weak to do it on this dark road. The river is a dull murmur in the back of my head, the creak a bare whisper.

Gran is dying, still, held in stasis in a brightly lit hospital bed. Is Owen with her? Did he call Gerry, and are they sitting there together comparing notes on these last few days? What will they say when they see me? There's probably still a bullet in my leg somewhere, and my lip is split, and one of my eyes is swollen closed. There's no explaining this away.

We reach the bottom of the driveway, and walk the thirty yards or so of Mountain Road to the gravel access road where I hid my truck. Amey lets me go then, and I sink to the edge of the pavement gratefully. The road is narrow here, unlined, the edges crumbling into the stream below, one of the unnamed feeders that meander down the mountain before dropping into something bigger. Marie sits down beside me, and Amey starts the long walk up the gravel road by herself. I waste a moment of worry for my truck, which is a manual transmission and lacking good power steering, but Amey has driven it before, and there's no way I'm getting back up that mountain, much less manipulating a clutch with a hole in my leg.

Marie and I are silent for a while, but it's a long wait. Eventually, she breaks it.

"You came alone," she says. "I couldn't have done that."

I don't say anything. There's a limit to how much of me I can give, and I've given it all tonight. Even politeness can't goad me into replying. Marie doesn't need it, though. She keeps going.

"I don't think I'll ever forgive you," she says. "Isn't that a mess? He hit me so many times. Locked Amey and me up. He was going to burn her because she'd tried to convince me to leave him. I even told her no, but that wasn't ever good enough. Being loyal wasn't ever good enough for him. He said he could see I loved her.

"And you know what else? I do." She goes quiet then, and I think she's done. She's not, though.

"How did he die?"

I run my hand through my short hair. There's blood caked in some of the strands, and who knows how that happened. A twig tumbles free.

"He drowned," I say at last. It sounds so impersonal. "I drowned him."

She takes in a breath, sharp. I hear it shudder out of her a moment later.

"Thank you," she says, so soft I can hardly hear it.

Then the truck's rumble cuts through the night noises, and the headlights are in our eyes.

I don't look at her, even though I want to, but I can feel her eyes on me.

We go home first, and in the truck, sitting down with the road spooling out under our wheels, I finally tell Amey about Gran.

She has to pull off the road once I do. The driver's-side door flies open, and Amey tumbles out to retch in the grass. Marie casts me a wide-eyed, unreadable look before she goes out after her. I hear Amey sob, and I hear Marie murmur something. I don't look. I stare at the road, which leads to the river, and I wonder if it will call my bones soon, and I don't feel anything about that. There's nothing left to feel. I've gone through grief, and I've gone through guilt and anger, too. It's too dark in this truck for hope just yet, so I wait.

Amey gets back in and keeps driving.

I left the back door standing open, nothing but a screen between the house and outside, which I discover only after we come in the mostly unused front door. Amey has to throw her shoulder in to pop it open where the house has settled over the years, which is why we mostly don't use it, but there's no way I'm getting up stairs. Amey helps me around the front and back into the bathtub at my insistence. Marie goes to boil a set of strong tweezers from the first aid kit and a knife while Amey gets the peroxide.

"We could take you to the hospital," Amey says, for the third time.

"And have to explain a bullet wound?" I say. "Everybody knows we don't hunt." I peel free of my jeans with a hiss, feeling skin tear and flesh strain. The wound is oozing, even with me telling the blood in emphatic terms that it is to stay where it is. Too much trauma. I contemplate it. "You got a cauterizing wand in there still?"

"Rhia," Amey says.

"Look, Amey. We both killed someone. And Randy's buried up in the woods, in case you're wondering, but the minute the sheriff puts two and two together, we are dead women walking. I've been through a lot tonight, and a hot bit of metal is not going to do me in."

I'm talking through my teeth, and we both know it, false bravado in the face of something I have no clue if I can handle, but I'm also right. I don't get to savor it long. Amey sits me in the bathtub and pours peroxide over the meat of my thigh and the small hole where the bullet's gone deep. Then Marie comes back with the tweezers.

I pull the bullet out myself, because I don't trust Marie to do it, and I don't want to put Amey through it, and it's the hardest thing I've ever done. The world spins and sparkles when I'm through, and I can't hold onto the blood anymore. It does what blood does. I'm glad I had the foresight to sit in the bathtub even though I'm not sure how much longer I'm going to be able to keep my head up.

Amey swabs the wound out with iodine, which somehow hurts more than the pliers did, and I scream, and bite down on the scream, and then Marie hands her the cauterizing wand, and I have a moment to take a breath, and then it's in my leg, and my scream becomes the real thing. It happens so fast, but I manage to hold my leg steady even though all I want to do is kick her. The bathroom smells of blood and cooked meat.

"Did I get it?" she says, and I can't tell who she's asking because I am floating somewhere far away.

"I think so," Marie answers after a moment.

They pop me full of Tylenol then, and make me eat something with it, even though all I feel like is throwing up. Amey helps me get up and wipes me down with a wet rag before they bind up the leg. I can feel, distantly, the blood moving the way it's supposed to, like a song from another room. I wonder if I have missed my calling as a doctor, and snort.

"What's so funny?" Amey says, out of breath from holding me up.

"You'll make a good nurse, Amey." She wrinkles her nose. I help her drag a nightdress over my head and put me in bed.

Then I sleep.

~

In my dreams, Gran and I are sitting on the porch.

"You did good, Rhia," she says. When I catch the look of her out of the corner of my eye, I see the tube that keeps her breathing, the IV lines, and the monitors. But when I look at her head on, she's just Gran. Her blue eyes are clearer than they've been in years.

"I'm sorry I didn't save you," I tell her.

"I was going to go eventually," Gran says. "We all do."

I wake up in my bed, and for a moment, I don't remember anything. There's sun on the walls, and birds singing outside.

Then I turn my head, and see Gerry lying on top of the covers next to me.

She's asleep, but she wakes when I shift, startling up.

"Rhia," she says, "are you okay?"

I snort a laugh, though there's not much humor in it.

"Did Amey call you?" I say instead of answering.

"Yeah," she says. "Rhia, what happened? Amey won't tell me anything, but you're a mess, and she and Marie look like they've been through the wringer, too."

"Less you know the better," I say, and she glares at me.

"This got anything to do with the fire up at Jack's place?"

My heart stutters at that. "Fire?" I ask, hoping I sound casual.

"Whole mountain is burning," Gerry says. "The police say it's a good thing that Marie is down here with you. Amey told them you were sick. They can't get up there to see what's going on, but Jack and Randy are missing. Folks in town are saying Randy and Jack finally got into it, though. Guess we'll know when the fire dies."

"I don't know anything about mountains burning," I say, mouth dry. The fire won't do too much damage to the forest, probably. The big trees will weather it, but I think of the bonfire, and how we left it. It was not a kind thing to do, and I hope the forest will forgive us for it. But it's the best thing that could have happened where Jack is concerned.

"Is there water?" I ask, changing the subject. "I've got to get dressed."

I struggle to sit up. Feels like every muscle in my body is sore, but my leg doesn't twinge as strongly as it should. I take the water Gerry gives me, drain it down, and feel instantly better.

"Here," Gerry says, holding up a jar that smells strongly of lavender and other healing herbs. "Amey said I should put this on your face."

"I've got it," I say, reaching for the jar and setting it on the bedside table. "Give me a minute to get dressed and all."

"Amey said," Gerry begins. I smile up at her wryly.

"Gerry, since when is Amey the one who has sense?"

"Since she's not the one with a face the color of one of my Cherokee Purples," Gerry snarks back, but she sighs and leaves, closing the door behind her.

I kick off the covers. Peel the bandage off my leg. The bullet hole is mostly closed, all scar tissue and scabs. I stare at it, feeling as if the world is tilting beneath me. The river chuckles in my chest. I know it healed me, then, and fear spikes before I can smother it. There will be a cost for all of this.

"Alright," I say, accepting it, letting the feeling fade. I'll pay when it comes time, just as I said I would.

Then I get up, slowly to keep my head from spinning, and put on a pair of jeans and a button-down flannel. I'm not sure I can keep my balance if I pull something over my head and there's a wrenching flame of pain in my shoulder from who knows what, and I don't want the pressure on my still-aching face.

"Where's Amey?" I ask when I've opened the bedroom door. Gerry leans on the doorframe, her curls still mussy from her nap on the bed. I wonder what time she got here, how long she watched me sleep.

"She went to see your Gran," Gerry says. "I'm supposed to take you, when you're ready."

"Did you," I begin, but I don't know how to finish. Gerry nods anyway.

"Owen called me last night. After you'd left." She looks up then, meets my eyes. "I'm not happy with you, Rhiannon Blackburn. I know you've always kept your secrets, but you—"

She looks away then.

I stand up, cross to her, and wrap my arms around her because it's what I have.

"It isn't about not trusting you, Gerry. I know you. You'd move heaven and earth for us."

"I know that," she says, hugging me back. "I know you've got your reasons. But I'm still mad."

She lets me go. I can't blame her for being angry at me. I smile, and she smiles, and she says, "Never do that again."

"Alright," I say, and mean it.

~

I spend more time than usual getting ready to go. My bullet wound may be miraculously healed but my face got pretty beat up last night, and that is still very apparent when I look in the mirror. I borrow Amey's concealer and foundation, even though it's not quite the right color, because I really don't want to see people's horrified expressions when they look at my black eye. The swelling has gone down more than it probably should have, but that purple-red is something I'd be less surprised to find on a painter's canvas. Gerry loans me a large pair of sunglasses because even after the makeup goes on, it still looks like I got knocked around. There's nothing I can do about the split lip, but the black eye will hopefully be a little less obvious.

Then we climb into Gerry's car, and I try not to think about where we are going. I'm not very successful. It's a long drive to the hospital.

The river and the creek both have been blessedly quiet all morning besides that chuckle about my leg. It makes it easier to sit in silence, to watch the road go by and contemplate things that need doing. I've got commissions I'm behind on, and who knows what's happening with the bills this month. My garden likely has tomatoes that need picking, probably the last of the year. Gerry stops on the way to pick up pizza, since it's nearing noon. We don't talk much until we're almost there, and then I find myself coming again and again to a thought I need to say.

"I wish there was some way to fix her," I tell Gerry. There are tears in my eyes behind my glasses, but I'm a water witch, and I'm tired of crying. They don't fall.

"I know, querida," she says.

We walk in the hospital, and Gerry leads me through the halls to the room they've got Gran in. Everything's white like I remember, but it doesn't feel so glaring now. It's not that I am stronger. It's that I know my own strength. I walk through the halls with a heavy heart, but I don't let that break me.

Amey and Marie are there, which I expected. I don't expect Owen.

He looks up at me, and I see him see the sunglasses and the bruises they're hiding. I see the anger and concern, and the way he smooths it off his face because right now is not the time. I don't think he's going to just clamp down on his questions like Gerry has, and I am not sure I want him to. But my heart twists in fear anyway, and hope. It's a stupid, fluttering thing, but there it is.

Amey gets up and hugs me then, breaking our eye contact. Marie comes over to Gerry and walks out with her, taking the pizza with them. Owen stands, too, and Amey lets go of me long enough to let me thank him, quietly, and promise to meet him soon.

"Take your time," he says, brushing my cheek lightly where the bruise peeks out from under the glasses. It hurts, just a little, but I know he doesn't mean it to. I grab his hand and squeeze. Then he leaves.

I take Amey's hand and cross to Gran.

"The doctor says she isn't coming back," Amey whispers to me, like saying it louder will make it true. I squeeze her hand, then wrap an arm around her. She's taller than me, but she's always been younger, and she's weeping now, breathing in soft gasps. I would bet that she hasn't cried before now. There was too much to feel and not enough time to feel it.

Now it's just the three of us, and the machines. There's no need to hold it in anymore. She turns and buries her face in my neck and sobs, and I'm glad that her feet aren't touching the ground, and I'm glad, too, that she loves me enough to cry on my shoulder.

The machines beep, and my sister, my blood cousin, my friend, sobs into my chest until she's empty. Then I make her meet my eyes.

"She is proud of you," I tell her, because I know it's true.

Amey nods. Closes her eyes.

"I'm ready," she says, and I don't have to ask her what she means.

I take off my glasses then, look at Gran with my own eyes. It's hard to see her so small, eyes closed, chest pumping from the ventilator as her body tries to gasp on. I swallow, grip Amey's hand tightly. Remember the wind in the trees, the touch of her hand on my hair, the smell of her.

"Gran," I say, reaching out with my free hand, grasping her cool, fragile fingers with my own. "I got her. I brought her home. It's okay."

There is a moment of stillness, as if even the machines have forgotten to move. The beeps that track her heart merge together into one long tone.

When the nurse comes running in, we tell her that Gran is gone, and there's no point in trying to bring her back. She's flown.

CHAPTER NINE

IT TAKES three days to plan the funeral. Gran had left some notes, mostly things she didn't want. A fancy casket was on the list, so the simple wooden box we carry out to the grave is notable only for the gleam of its polish. I couldn't have handled poorly worked wood.

There's a preacher in from the Unitarian church in the town over. Poor man had a devil of a time not looking at my black eye while he interviewed us about what to say. He's not a terrible speaker, and there's no blood or brimstone in it, which I like. Amey insists on releasing a dove, which I roll my eyes at, but it's Amey, and she loves her birds. It is kind of nice, watching the white wings beat at the air.

There's a lot of people who have come from when Gran was working, and some of Amey's friends, and Gerry's family. Owen is there, and he sits with me by the grave after all the glad-handing is done. I'm picking apart a lily, tossing the petals one by one on the coffin, my black suit heavy and hot in the sunlight. I would have preferred rain for a funeral, but Gran always did love sunny, brisk days. Amey and Marie are not far away, saying goodbye to Gerry. I've already said my goodbyes. I'm just not ready to leave.

The smell of lilacs brings my head up.

"What is it?" Owen asks. I cast my eyes all around. The wind is coming from the east, opposite of where Amey and Marie are standing, and I get up and walk that way without answering Owen, eyes straining.

There, in the shadows of an old oak tree, I think I see a familiar shape. A man, stuck forever in his prime, suspenders holding his pants on his skinny waist. There's someone with him. She has black hair, striped with silver, and as I watch, she turns around and looks at me. Waves, once.

Then the wind gusts. I blink my eyes.

They're gone.

Owen comes up behind me.

"Rhia, are you okay?"

I turn, look at him. The scent of lilacs tickles my nose, overwhelms, momentarily, the scent of lilies.

"Yeah," I say. "Yeah, I am." Then I smile, because I'm glad he's here.

We walk back to where Amey and Marie are waiting, and if I look back over my shoulder once, who can blame me? What comes before makes you. But only you get to decide where you're going.

ACKNOWLEDGMENTS

This book would not have been possible without a whole passel of people.

First, a special thanks to my editor, Holly, for her work in bringing this book to life. Thanks also to Lee Murray for giving it a chance as acquisitions editor. It's always so wonderful to work with other creators, and I'm very grateful to Interstellar Flight Press for providing a home for Rhia's story.

Family is at the heart of this book, and my own family inspired this story in a number of ways. Thanks to my Mom and Dad for dragging us all back to live on the riverbank all those years ago. Thanks, too, to my grandparents and great-grandparents, who are mostly gone now but whose stories and choices continue to influence my life. None of them will ever read these words, but I owe them a debt of gratitude, even the ones I never knew and probably wouldn't get along with.

In Rhia's story, several places and communities from Southwest Virginia have been mushed together. Names have been changed to protect the innocent and to account for that creative license. My love for this place is as conflicted as Rhia's, if in different ways. Appalachia has a dense and complicated history. While that is not the focus of this book, the long history of disinvestment in this area and the scars left by choices largely outside of the control of people who live here cannot be understated. There are critiques to level, but there's also a great deal of learning to be done.

I want to thank Mike Allen for listening to me rant about writing and for publishing my earlier novella, "Viridian"; Laura Blackwell, for reading an early draft of this book not long after it was written and loving it; the folks at Futurescapes 2018 for all their feedback on early pages of this story; and to Nevada for betaing. Also, thanks to the Inklings group chat for your publishing insights, and to C.S.E. Cooney for cheering me on as I wrestled with being a new mom while trying to maintain some writing momentum.

Lastly, thanks to my long-suffering husband for always tackling the dishes, especially on nights when I ignore him for a book, and to my son. You're a star, and I hope you read this someday.

ABOUT THE AUTHOR

Amanda J. McGee is a planner by day and a writer by night. She has degrees from Hollins University and Virginia Tech, where she studied languages, identity politics, policy, and infrastructure. She is the author of the dark epic fantasy series The Creation Saga and is an Art Matters Grant recipient, a program of the City of Roanoke and the National Endowment for the Arts. Her novella *Viridian* was published in the anthology *A Sinister Quartet*, which made the 2020 Locus Recommended Reading List. *A River Wide* is her debut standalone novella.

When not writing, Amanda can be found reading books or hiking mountains, depending on the season. She lives in Southwest Virginia with the love of her life, her son, two fluffy cats, and a plethora of plants. You can find out more on her website at http://amandajmcgee.com.

ABOUT THE COVER ARTIST

Dante Luiz is an illustrator and occasional writer from an island in southern Brazil. He's the interior artist for *Crema* (*comiXology/Dark Horse*), and his work with comics has also appeared in anthologies, like *Wayward Kindred (TO Comix Press), Mañana: Latinx Comics From the 25th Century (Power & Magic Press),* and *Shout Out (TO Comix Press)*, among others. Find him online at danteluiz.com

x.com/dntlz

instagram.com/dntlz

INTERSTELLAR FLIGHT PRESS

Interstellar Flight Press is an indie speculative publishing house. We feature innovative works from the best new writers in science fiction and fantasy. In the words of Ursula K. Le Guin, we need "writers who can see alternatives to how we live now, can see through our fear-stricken society and its obsessive technologies to other ways of being, and even imagine real grounds for hope."

Find us online at www.interstellarflightpress.com.

www.ingramcontent.com/pod-product-compliance
Lightning Source LLC
Chambersburg PA
CBHW031013080926
51115CB00028B/609